Scorn and Sorrow

Adventures of a Villain-Leaning Humanoid

Book 3

Jamie Jackson

CONTENT/TRIGGER WARNINGS

Psychic/mental coercion, blood & gore, harsh language, sex and sexual situations, sexual assault

CONTENTS

ACKNOWLEDGMENTS

Once again, I thank my family for putting up with me. I wouldn't be where I am today without you.

Thank you to Jennifer, for believing in this series, and continuing to help me breathe life into it.

CHAPTER ONE

Oh look, you're back. I thought you would be. In case you need it, I'm Megaera, Meg for short, and last time on our misadventures we ran into a hero who was immune to my power of fear and ended up battling a villain who could not only make rats do his bidding but mutate them into zombies and giant monsters. And that jerk shot me. Which did not hurt as much as I was expecting it to.

Oh, yeah, also, I died, but I got better. Thanks to the hero with immunity. Oh, and Virgil. He deserves some credit.

And I still don't know what Greg is hiding in his sock drawer.

Ready? Good.

Here we go.

∞

Greg and I were arguing.

"I just don't see why we would need—"

"You don't see how it would be convenient if you could just—"

"It's a weak point! Anyone could gain entry—"

"How many other people do you know who can fly?"

"My dad for starters," he snapped.

"Oh."

"Yeah."

I paused to think for a minute. We were standing in what was going to be our new base of operations, but because it was still under construction, we had the option to make things exactly the way we wanted. The skyscraper was already towering; beams and girders, rebar and concrete, bare studs, wires and pipes formed a giant, empty room that currently had open holes where the windows would go and a balcony. Oh yeah, up on the top floor too. Which, you might be thinking, who the fuck puts a balcony on a building that goes fifty stories or higher up?

Heroes do. Especially when the hero handling the approval of the blueprints was Virgil and he agreed with me that a balcony would be practical for Greg. My fear of heights aside, it just made sense to suggest our apartment have one, so he could take off straight from home.

Apparently one of Virgil's clients is a real estate developer, and while Virgil is miffed that we will be sharing our base with offices, we do get the top six floors all to ourselves. Virgil managed to get the real estate developer to hire the same contractor who had built the military's hero building to ensure we had access to the same materials. Supposedly the contractor is under the impression that Virgil's client is very eccentric and convinced that someone is out to kill him. Which, eh, could be true anyway.

Either way, we're getting the same not-glass for the windows, and he had promised he could get the balcony doors made out of it too. So why wouldn't we do that? It's better than Greg having to waste time jogging up to the roof or down to the street every time he leaves.

Okay, yeah, we get to have our own private elevator, and I'm going to have to get over my elevator prejudices because I cannot be climbing up and down fifty plus stories every time we're in a rush.

I'm getting off track; I was in the middle of trying to

make a point.

"I still think that having the balcony would be worth it. We'll just lock the doors."

"Lock the doors?" Greg was making that strangled sound again. "We'll just lock the doors."

"Think of how much faster you can make it to my rescue if all you have to do is run out and jump over the railing."

He was scrubbing at his face, shoving his blond hair back.

"You won't have to waste time racing up or down the stairs," I wheedled.

"We have an elevator."

"Still faster to be able to take off right there," I said, pointing at the balcony. "Also, I bet you Virgil can get the contractor to install something that'll lock the door down so it can't be opened."

He was vacillating; I could see it in his dark brown eyes, and if I hadn't been in the equation, he probably would've already agreed to having it. I was trying to figure out how to press my advantage without pulling out the big guns. Use those too often and they lose their effect.

I slipped my arms around his waist and stepped forward so I was pressed against his chest, head tilted back so I could look him in the face. "I absolutely promise to always lock down the door if I'm in our apartment by myself."

He sighed, wrapped his arms around me and kissed the top of my head. Ha! I win!

"That is cheating," he said.

"How is that cheating?" I protested. Now we were going to have a new argument? "I just promised to lock the door."

"I know exactly what you were saying, and that's cheating." But there was amusement in his voice. "Fine, tell Virgil to leave the fucking balcony."

Also, no, that's not the big gun.

Greg had moved on and was examining the tape

marking out spaces on the floor. His brow furrowed. He pointed at one end of the room. "What's going over there?"

"I don't know. A bathroom?"

"There's no plumbing over there. The plumbing is on that side."

Now I was looking at the tape too, trying to figure it out. "I thought we were doing another studio-with-loft combo?"

"Yes."

"So why the extra room?" I mean, even I could tell it was an extra room because someone had helpfully marked DOOR on the tape, and the door was inside the space we were standing in, so the entry wasn't going to be from the hall. It couldn't be space for Virgil's lab because that was supposed to be getting its own floor anyway.

We were both silent, stymied by whatever was going over there.

"I'm going to ask Virgil," Greg said pulling out his phone, which immediately began ringing. Greg narrowed his eyes and answered it. "What's going in the marked off space in our apartment?"

I snorted. "Not even a hello." Greg shot me a look and held up a finger. Point to me!

Oh yeah, Greg and I have a new game where we predict what Virgil is going to say when one of us is on the phone with him.

So far, I'm winning. No, it's not because the only one of us Virgil calls is Greg. Okay, yes, it totally is why.

"Space for future use," Greg continued, sounded dubious. "What kind of future use?"

"Is he going to make us babysit clients directly in our apartment?" I interrupted.

Greg nodded.

"Where's my point?"

He covered the speaker. "He didn't say it in those words."

"That should count! Ooh, still on the phone!" I said.

Greg rolled his eyes and held up another finger. "Uh huh, I'll tell her. What's the plan with the balcony?"

Oh, we're back to this now. I crossed my arms and glared at him. "I bet you he already knows I won that one." I mean, he would probably override Greg winning the argument anyway. Because I know for a fact that he had already taken making sure the door could be locked down into account.

Okay, yeah, technically I cheated to win that argument. But not via wheedling and taking safety seriously promises like Greg thinks.

Greg scrubbed at his face again. "Yeah, no, it's fine. It makes sense. Yup, we'll be back in a bit." He hung up.

"Something going on?"

"No, nothing we need to handle. Ranger's already on it. Virgil just doesn't like not having one of us on site."

We were already living in the city itself, in temporary quarters essentially. Even Virgil had been getting exasperated by the amount of time it would take to get all of us downtown for a call when we were still living at his compound in the middle of nowhere. So, his client gave us housing while we wait for the real base to get constructed.

It was driving Greg nuts because the reinforcement he wanted was most definitely not there. But he couldn't argue the convenience of it.

Ranger, on the other hand, was loving it and kept offering to take us clubbing.

So far, he hasn't brought anyone he's met back to the apartments. Virgil might murder him if he did. But there are definitely nights where he doesn't come back until four or so in the morning, which wouldn't be remarkable in and of itself, but those times he smells very strongly of perfume.

I don't know who he's seeing those nights, but they need to stop applying scents like eighty-year-old ladies. It makes me sneeze, so I refuse to be around him until he's showered.

Greg is totally okay with those mornings because it means I shut the door in Ranger's face.

Yeah, no, they only kind of get along. Mission-wise, they're both all business. And Ranger might have stopped actively trying to step in between us, but he still flirts with me on occasion, and he'll still do it in front of Greg. Virgil said he's not sure Ranger knows how to shut it off.

Which, bullshit. But he's not chasing me around, so I mostly ignore him. And he's stopped making snide comments about Greg altogether.

"So, tell me what?" I asked.

"It's supposed to be a panic room for clients," Greg said.

"Why does it have to be in our apartment?"

"He's putting one in all the apartments."

Well, fine then. Greg slid an arm around my waist. "You ready to go?" he asked, steering me toward the balcony. I didn't answer until we were standing on it. We've got a pretty nice view from here; I can see the harbor. Well, kind of. There's a lot of other buildings around, but I've got a view of a sliver of it, and I'm getting better about the heights thing. What is it the studies say? Repeated exposures to the phobia can cure it? So I'm either cured, or as a survival mechanism, my brain has decided not to care so I don't drop dead from a heart attack. Or is that the same as being cured?

The flex of his fingers against my hip made me realize I hadn't actually answered him yet. "Yup," I said.

He scooped me up and jumped over the railing.

∞

I woke up before Greg the next morning. I slid out of bed, and even after I was showered and dressed, he was still asleep, one arm flung across my side of the bed, hair mussed and in his face.

My eyes followed the line of muscle down his arm, along his broad shoulders, down his back, and then I took the opportunity to sneak out.

Don't give me that look, Jesus, I left him a note. I'm

only going out to get coffee. Do you have any idea how hard it is to sneak off to get surprises for someone who can hear every move you make? I mean, I can't even get breakfast in bed done before he's awake. Something about all the clattering. Which might be on purpose because then he nudges me out of the kitchen. You can't tell me you've never tossed around some pots and pans because you're hungry and *somebody* isn't awake yet.

Also, I still manage to burn boiled eggs. Greg's trying to teach me how to cook, but now he's extra nervous about it. I cut myself on the chef knife, and if Ranger hadn't been inside at the time to reverse the damage, I would've needed stitches.

Either way, I left our current apartment building and headed for the coffee shop up the block. Seriously, Ranger is right, city living is the way to go. I don't know how I managed to stand being in Virgil's compound for so long. There's nothing to do there.

Okay, I don't go anywhere anyway. Not the point. I like the option. To do nothing. Shut up.

The only downside to the city is all the people. Of course, this coffee shop is always busy, no matter what time of day. Greg says it's because they make good lattes. So, there I was, waiting in line behind a woman with cherry red hair bright against the rich brown of her skin, half of the tightly curled coils bobbed, the other half shaved.

Man, I never do anything fun with my own hair. Thick, black with bouncy ringlets, its choices are up or down. Maybe I should get a cut. Although I definitely like the shiver I get when Greg puts his hands in it, so maybe I should leave it.

Oh wait, I'm here for coffee. Mind out of the gutter.

But that thought just brought me back around to the last time he had his hands in my hair, fingers gently tangled in the curls, his lips brushing along the skin of my neck down to my collarbone...

Obviously, I was mildly distracted when someone got in line behind me.

The whispers were calling me, trying to get my attention, which put me on alert. I could feel my shoulders tense, because how was I supposed to look behind me without putting the person on notice that I knew something was up? If I couldn't come back to my favorite coffee shop because I had to murder someone, I was going to be pissed.

You know, a lot of my stories seem to start with people getting into my personal space. What is up with that?

I didn't have to say anything because he spoke first.

"Megaera?" The question was said in the tone of pleasant surprise, but the voice was gravelly and harsh, like you would hear from someone who had ruined their vocal cords from years of yelling, not quite a smoker's voice but maybe smoke from something else. The whispers said, *look*, so I turned. The man behind me was burly, the confident stance of someone who knew how to handle himself in a fight, the steely-eyed squint of a combat veteran, brown hair in a buzz cut. Absently, I registered that his eyes were grey, like mine. Stormy.

I see the same look in Greg and Virgil's eyes sometimes, too. It makes me wonder what they've seen to give them that expression.

The eyes gave me a familiar, assessing flick.

Oh, fuck no, he did not. My hackles up now, I growled. "What?"

He didn't seem bothered by my tone. "I don't recall you being quite so small in stature."

"Well, I don't recall you at all, so back up out of my space," I snapped.

"Now that approach I do recall. Always the first one over the wall. Nice to know some things don't change." He put a hand on my elbow. "Come, we have much to discuss, and this is not the place for it."

I yanked my arm away, and instead of calling the whispers, I chose to get loud. "Excuse you, but I don't know you, so don't touch me."

Sometimes you need the help of the general public.

My shouting attracted attention, people in the coffee shop turning to stare at us.

His stance didn't change, the eyes still cool and measuring. "If you'll listen—"

"Hey, jackass," said Cherry Hair from behind me now, "she said she don't know you. Back off."

He transferred his gaze to her. "Or you'll what? Call your police?"

"No, I'll just light you on fire. So back off."

He paused, eyes roving between the two of us, and he looked like he was calculating his odds. Finally, he nodded and moved his eyes back to my face. "When you decide to be reasonable, find me on the battlefield." And he left.

The battlefield? What the fuck did that even mean? I was going to have to stop leaving the apartment altogether. I kept getting approached by melodramatics. But I had never been one to investigate mysterious circumstances, and riddles were even worse.

The volume in the coffee shop that had dropped considerably started to pick back up, the entertainment over.

I turned to Cherry Hair. "Thanks."

She shrugged. "Ladies gotta stick together. Fucking weirdos everywhere." Her brown eyes gave me a quick gauging glance. "Hero work, huh?"

I snorted. "I stick out that much?"

"Yup, it's the shoulders. And you're balanced on the balls of your feet." She held out a hand. "I'm Maniac."

I took it, a quick shake. "Vengeance."

"That's not what that dude called you."

"Given name," I said grudgingly. Her eyes widened a fraction.

"Oooh, wait, you're Meg, aren't you?"

Damn it. Does everyone know about me? "Yes," I sighed.

She grinned. "Since we're sharing, I'm Cecilia. Only Cecilia, never Cece. That's a burning offense."

9

∞

Maniac and I ended up having coffee together. I texted Greg to let him know I had been delayed and that if he wanted to join me when he got up, I would probably still be here.

We both avoided any stories about things we had done in the line of duty. Guess she gets enough hero talk too.

But she was telling me about the time she took a road trip down South and tried boiled peanuts for the first time. I was in stitches over her description of the guy manning the stall; she could do a perfect imitation of his accent.

"He kept calling me 'ma'am!' And I'm like, do I look like a ma'am to you? And he's all, 'Yes ma'am, you look like a ma'am. As far as I can tell, you're a lady. You got parts I don't know about?' And I was like, well you're definitely not gonna find out what parts I do have."

I was giggling like mad. "You did not."

"Oh, I absolutely did." She looked at the door, and the smile fell off her face and her skin went grey.

A hand on my shoulder, and I twisted my head to look up at Greg, who was glaring stony-faced at her.

"Hey there, Fortress," she said.

"Maniac," he said, tersely. "Who've you set fire to lately?"

"Your hair grew back," she said defensively. "Not like you can get damaged anyway."

I could hear an air of menace in his tone. "What about the others who were in the building?"

She coughed. "They were fine. No one died."

"That time," he snapped.

"Hey, I changed sides, shouldn't that earn me some leniency?"

"No, I don't think it should." I could feel his fingers flex against me.

"Well," she said. "This reunion has been incredibly awkward. We should all hang out some time. Catch you around Meg." She got up to go.

"No, you won't," he said.

She gave the two of us a cool appraisal, responding before I could. "Yeah? I feel like she might have her own opinions on who she chills with." I could feel Greg's fingers flex again, but he didn't respond. She gave him another beat before she said anything else. "Like I said, catch you around."

I waited until she was out the door. "What was that about?" I demanded.

"She is — she *was* a villain," Greg grunted.

"Yeah, I got that part. Care to explain further?"

He scrubbed at his face, grabbed the empty cup she had left on our table and tossed it in the trash along with mine. "Not here and not now. Virgil wants to see us. Come on."

"You could've texted that to me."

"I was hoping to grab coffee with you first."

"We could still get coffee."

"Not in the mood."

"For coffee or coffee with me?"

He paused, moved his hand to the back of my neck. "I'm always in the mood for coffee with you." He pulled me up out of my seat with his free hand. "Come on. Virgil first, coffee later."

∞

Virgil was pacing the floor of his makeshift lab and security room when we got back. He had removed his jacket, leaving the duster draped over the back of a chair, his t-shirt clinging to his whipcord frame, and the abstract sleeve tattoos clearly visible on his arms. One arm was crossed over his chest, his other hand up at his dark brown beard. He had managed to set up cameras so that he had views of everyone coming and going in the building, as well as the sidewalk and alleys outside, even the elevator and hallway of our floor.

Greg took a minute to eye the equipment. "When did

you set all this up?"

"Last night. We don't have any additional protections in place right now, and I don't like not knowing who's around us."

"Hmm," Greg said. "Is this why you wanted to see us?"

"No." Virgil was over at the monitors waving his hand, and the item in view kept switching until it came up on the one he wanted. "There."

It was a view from within a museum. The camera was centered on an exhibit related to ancient Greece.

"If this is a history lesson, can we go with a different location? I've had my fill of all things Greek," I said. I'm even prejudiced against the food at this point. Thanks, Mom and Dad.

What? You already knew I'm petty. Get over it.

"Not a history lesson. Watch," Virgil said. We watched. Well, Virgil and Greg watched, I was busy rolling my eyes. Nothing happened for a long moment, and then movement on the screen recaptured my attention as something slithered out of one of the statues. Several more followed it.

"Snakes," I said.

"Why did it have to be snakes?" Ranger intoned from the door. He was leaning against the frame, arms crossed. He had left his leather jacket unzipped, exposing the black t-shirt underneath. His own dark brown eyes were focused on the screen, and unlike Greg, he keeps his black hair cut short so it's not constantly flopping in his face and if I think I look constantly tan due to my olive tone skin, Ranger's got me beat.

Greg scrubbed his face. "Why do we have to deal with animals at all? What happened to the good old days of bank robberies and run of the mill villains?"

"You'd rather deal with high-speed flight chases?" Virgil asked.

"Absolutely. The last time we had animals it was rats. *Giant* rats."

"Don't forget the zombie ones," I told him. Greg shot me a glare.

"What, you got a problem with rats?" Ranger asked.

"I have a problem with them when they're being mutated. Those things weren't trying to bite you."

"You afraid of rats, Greg?" Ranger smirked.

Oh good, we're back to the snide comments.

Virgil cleared his throat. "If you're quite done. Someone needs to go make sure the snakes are nothing. That statue is a piece I'm familiar with, and there's nowhere a snake, let alone five or six of them, could've gotten into it."

"On it," Ranger said.

"Take Meg with you," Virgil said. Next to me, Greg stiffened.

Ranger was still leaning languidly against the door, but I could feel his interest sharpen. "Why? It's just snakes."

"Because her power talks to her and regularly notices things ahead of the rest of us. That's why."

"She's still not outfitted—" Greg started to argue.

"One, they're going during the day while the museum is open. It's unlikely that anything is going to happen. Two, she'll be outfitted by this afternoon. The polythene fiber is in. I sincerely doubt anything that she and Ranger can't handle will crop up in between."

Greg was grinding his teeth, but he didn't have anything he could use to win against Virgil's logic. Not without making me mad. He was working hard not to let his inclinations to keep me protected override his common sense, and I could hardly blame him for finding it difficult to do. Especially since last time I was out of his sight while on a mission I kind of died. After a moment of uncomfortable silence, he switched topics.

"I have news for you."

"Oh?" Virgil asked.

"Maniac is back."

"Interesting. She's going to find working in this town tricky, what with the target on her back." Virgil turned back towards the monitors. "The motivation from that might be particularly useful."

Greg scowled. "If you approach her, keep me out of it."

"No guarantees," Virgil said. "Ranger, Meg, get going. The museum is opening in less than thirty minutes. You should be there right on time."

Ranger jerked his head. "On the bike, we'll be early." He headed out the door without waiting for Greg's glower.

Virgil vaguely waved a hand at us. "Go be cute somewhere else. I'm concentrating."

Greg and I stepped out and the door closed behind us, gently instead of Virgil's customary slam. Greg put a hand on my face, tipping my chin up as his head tilted down so our eyes could meet.

"You going to tell me what the whole Maniac thing is about?" I asked.

"I don't like her."

"Why not?" She hadn't seemed all that bad.

He sighed. "She was a villain. A lot of innocent people died when she was involved. Isn't that reason enough?" His eyes were sad, haunted, and I was afraid to ask what he had seen to make them look that way.

Maybe when he says he deals with enough blood during the day he's not just talking about the villains and monsters he has to kill.

I rose up on my toes and kissed him because I'm not the kind of person to talk through the trauma. I ignore it and hope for the best. He pulled me into him, hand on my back, one in my hair. I had twined my arms around his neck when someone cleared their throat. We broke apart.

"We're going to be late," Ranger said.

"Watch yourself," Greg told me.

"Always," I told him.

Yes, we've become that couple, with the code words for I love you. Shut up.

He kissed me again before he let me go so I could follow Ranger out the door.

CHAPTER TWO

With Ranger's driving, we were at the museum right on time. He left the bike parked at the curb.

"You don't worry about it getting towed?" I asked him.

"Nah. Any time they've done that I just go down to the impound lot and break it out."

We were climbing the steps to the museum, which had large, stone lions at either side at the top and soaring Corinthian columns at the front. In comparison to the façade, the glass doors to get in felt small, feeble, too weak to support the large gold vertical bars used to open them.

Ranger pulled the door open. "Ladies first."

"Why, so the monsters can get me first?"

He had one hand wrapped around the edge of the door, elbow cocked to keep it supported and open. "You know, you could just let me be polite to you."

"I don't think that would be on brand," I said, but I stepped past him to go inside. He followed, the door swinging shut behind him.

The interior of the museum stuck with the soaring theme. The ceiling looked like it went all the way to the roofline, and hung from it were displays of sharks and ancient sea creatures, including a plesiosaurus. Under the lifelike models sat the main desk, a circle of gleaming mahogany colored wood. Ranger bellied up to it like it was bar, leaning onto the desk like he was about to ask for two fingerfuls of whiskey.

"Yo," he said to the woman working the counter. She gave him a smile I was extremely familiar with faking. It was the tight customer service "*I have to smile at you so I don't get fired*" smile. I slipped in, using my elbow to startle him into a step back.

"Hi," I said. "Can we get two tickets please?"

"General admission, general with one special exhibit, or general plus all special exhibits?" Her smile seemed a little more genuine when it was directed at me.

Well, damn. I didn't know. I'm was pretty sure I hadn't been to a museum since grade school.

Ranger saved me from indecision. "General and all exhibits."

"That'll be sixty-six dollars please."

Ranger pulled out his wallet and handed over cash. She handed us two printed tickets. It was incredibly complicated and riveting.

"Maps of the museum are over there by the gift store," she said pointing it out. "Enjoy your visit."

"Wow," Ranger muttered as we headed over to the map stand. "They can't even keep them at the desk to give straight to you?"

I ignored him and pulled a map out, unfolding it to figure out where the Greek exhibit was. It was all the way to the right side of the building, so we were going to have walk through the dinosaurs, cavemen and Egyptian displays first. I started forward. "Come on, we need to go this way."

"You in a hurry?" Ranger asked. "Don't want to maybe take your time? Look around? We paid to get in here you know."

"I would like to get in, find out what's up with the snakes and leave."

"Why? So you can get back to the attack dog?"

I spun on my heel to face him. "What's it to you?"

"You know you two are allowed to have lives outside of each other, right? Relax on occasion? Have a little fun? See other friends? Jesus, not like that Meg, don't give me that look. I'm not hitting on you."

I couldn't argue the look I had given him, but I did have something I could argue, so I did. "For once."

He stepped around me. "I am not playing that game with you today. We can either have a nice morning poking around museum exhibits, or you can spend it pouting because I won't argue with you."

I opened my mouth to argue, then closed it because he was right, damn it.

"You spend it pouting and have a bad day, and you've only got yourself to blame," he told me from next to the Parasaurolophus.

I glowered at him, taking a moment to think. To his credit, he waited patiently for me to get over my snit. "Fine," I finally said. "But could we figure out the snake issue first and then poke around exhibits on the way back out?"

He grinned at me. "I think we can compromise on that."

We made our way to the Greek exhibit, but then we had to pause. Because we had to remember which statue the snakes had come from, and there were a lot of them.

I probably should've been paying more attention.

What? I'm still getting the hang of taking this whole hero thing seriously. What do you want from me?

"What do you remember about the statue?" I asked Ranger.

"It had no arms."

"That's all of them."

"Not true. That one has arms."

"It has *an* arm."

"One arm is more than no arms."

I tried not to laugh and failed. Ranger started to lean

against one of the statutes, and I snatched at him. "Don't do that! You'll get us kicked out!" Security was glaring over at us from his position across the room. Ranger was grinning, and I was giggling.

"Not into rule breaking, Meg?"

"Depends on how stupid the rule is."

"I feel like you find a lot of rules stupid."

"Not as many as you do, apparently. Illegal parking, grand theft auto…" We were circling around the statues, trying to gauge if any of them was the one we were looking for. Ranger paused by one and looked up at the ceiling.

"The camera is over there, so if we look at the angle, we could figure out which statue we need to be checking. And is it really theft if I'm just taking back my own bike?"

"You tell me. You're the one doing it."

Ranger was trying to gauge the camera to the statue distance without attracting the guard's attention again. "We need to go about two statues up and then three over." I followed him, and we came around the front of a statue that I hadn't seen from the door, the view of it blocked by a larger one of a man and woman standing together.

It was a man, and his expression wasn't one that was common to these types of statues. He looked surprised. Like that moment when something dangerous jumps out at you, the breath right before the fear hits you. The whispers plucked at me.

Ranger hadn't noticed that the statue didn't look right. He was busy circling it, looking for anywhere the snakes could have come from. "Hey, could they have come out of this base section?" I pulled my gaze away from the face and circled around with him.

"I don't see how. It looks like one solid piece to me. Most of these would have been carved from a single block of marble."

"Yeah?"

"Yeah," I said, still distracted by the face and the

whispers. "They wouldn't have left them white either, they would've been painted."

"You're just a fount of information. Know anything else about these things?"

"More than I would like to," I admitted. "The face isn't right."

"Not right how?"

"I haven't seen one like this before." I waved vaguely at the others. "Look at all of them, all the pieces of a single person, what do they look like to you?"

He looked around. "Hmm, serious, like attack dog does."

"Okay, if you're going to be like that I'm not—"

"Wait, wait! I'm sorry. I just meant, does he smile? He always looks serious; these statues look serious. It was the best example I could think of. What's the difference in the serious ones versus this guy?"

"That's just it, the only time I've seen anything other than *serene-*" and I emphasized the word, "is for action-related pieces, not the ones who are just - standing and minding their own business would be the best way to phrase it. But this guy, he was obviously just chilling. Look at him: his head is tilted back like he's looking at something looming over him. But he's still just standing there. Like he can't remember how to run." The whispers were agreeing with me, but they couldn't tell me why.

Ranger was watching me thoughtfully. "I think that's the most words I've ever heard you string together in one sitting."

"Yeah, because I purposely avoid having long, in-depth discussions with you."

"Ow," he said. "That hurts. No really, that hurts." But he was grinning at me.

"Are you done?" I asked.

"Oh, I've been done. I've been busy hanging on your every word."

I snorted, and turned away so I could hide my face while pretending to look at the other statues. Ranger was silent for a moment, his boots scuffing the floor behind me. Then he stepped past me, looking around at the floor. "What?" I asked him.

"I'm just trying to see if there's any evidence that there were snakes here other than the security tapes Virgil got a hold of. A piece of snakeskin or something. Some sort of trace they were here." The security guard seemed to have gotten tired of watching us and had moved on to another room.

We ended up splitting up so we could cover more ground of the room, and then Ranger called me over to a bench. When I got over to him, he reached under it and pulled out a snakeskin close to three feet in length.

"Oh gross," I said. What kind of custodians does this museum have that they missed that?

"It's fresh," Ranger said. "Still damp." He held it out toward me.

"I'm not touching that."

"Well, I'm taking it back to Virgil in case our snakes have anything they can tell him."

"I'm not touching that thing."

"I'm going to need both hands to drive the bike."

"Well then you're going to have wear it as a tie or something because I'm not touching that."

"Since when are you so squeamish?"

"Do I look outdoorsy to you? I'm not touching the snakeskin."

He was standing too close to me, looking down at my face, his expression serious. "You know, you should try expanding your horizons."

I took a step back. "To include what? Because I think they're good where they are."

"Things like camping, rock climbing, hiking. Outdoorsy things."

"You mean camping where you sleep on the ground?"

"Yes, camping where you sleep on the ground. You know you're in a tent for that right? Sleeping bags and things? You're not right on the ground."

"No thanks," I said. "I'm a city girl. I like the convenience of coffee right down the street that I haven't had to make myself. And things like mattresses. And not sleeping on the ground."

"And no trees. No stars, the air always smells like car exhaust—"

"You know you don't have to stay in the city with us if you don't want to."

"Oh, I didn't say I don't like city life. Just that sometimes it's nice to get away to somewhere where you have some windows."

"Okay," I said, because I was trying to end the conversation before it meandered somewhere I wasn't comfortable with.

"Okay you'll try camping?"

"I did not say that."

"I think you should try camping. Bring the attack dog with you. See how he does in the wilderness with the bears." He winked at me, then brought the snakeskin up and wiggled it too close to me for comfort, so I had to step back again. "Come on, we need to go take this to Virgil."

"I'm sorry, did you just say bears?"

"What about the bears?"

"I'm definitely never going camping."

"Oh, like a bear could get near you and the freaky shit you do."

I rolled my eyes and turned to head back toward the front of the museum. Ranger caught up to me, rolling the snakeskin up and tucking it inside his jacket. I caught a glimpse of the sleeve, the long tear from when we first met still there. He had reversed the other tears to fix the damage, so why not that one?

My phone pinged, distracting me from the thought. Not

that I would've asked Ranger about it anyway. I might get an answer I don't want to hear. It was a text from Greg: "It's getting late, want to do lunch instead of coffee when you get back? Taco truck is in the park." I smiled and texted back "yes."

Ranger was trying to peek over my shoulder. "You're all smiley now. It's attack dog, isn't it?"

I pulled my phone out of his view, turned off the screen and slipped it into the back pocket of my jeans. "Does it matter?"

We were meandering through the Egyptian exhibit now. They currently didn't have any mummies, just jewelry, furniture, photos of the pyramids and sphinx. Personally, I was glad they didn't have any mummies, because we had already fought enough strange creatures. I did not need to live through a mummy and his curse. Okay, they had mummified cats on display, but that's a little less creepy than displaying a person. I totally got why people think a mummy's curse is a real thing. It feels crazy disrespectful to display someone's body like that.

Hey, just because I rip people to pieces doesn't mean I don't have respect for the dead.

Ranger had paused to read an info card about Howard Carter. He snorted. "Fucking graverobbers." I came up next to him to figure out what he was talking about. I didn't see anything other than things about Carter and the excavation of Tutankhamun.

"What?" I asked him.

"People like him." He waved a hand. "Him and all those other historians. They claim they just want to know what people in the past were like, but they go in and steal national treasures. If they just wanted to know, they would excavate and then give these things to the local museums, not ship them halfway across the world so people like us can overpay to gape at them. And it's not just the big things; look at all the little things they take. Things people could see and feel closer to their ancestors through. Know how their ancestors lived, their braveries, their struggles, their culture."

"Hmm," I said. I didn't think he was wrong, but I had nothing to add to it. I don't do deep thoughts.

Ranger moved away from the display. "Come on, I'd rather look at the dinosaurs anyway. At least they don't care that they've been dug up."

∞

When we got back, Greg at least waited long enough for Ranger and me to tell Virgil what we found, which consisted of the snakeskin, and the whispers' vague assertion that something was off about the statue. But it most definitely didn't include anywhere the snakes could have come from.

Virgil rubbed the bridge of his nose. "I just don't see how snakes can pass through solid stone."

Ranger shrugged.

"We've seen weirder things," I said. "What about Red Eye? What he could do was weird." I could feel my heart speed up at mentioning him, but I squashed it down. Fuck him. He's dead. I won. And I will keep repeating that to myself. It's my mantra.

"And it shouldn't have been possible, I know." Virgil was in his thinking pose again, one arm crossed over his chest, hand up at his chin. "But it was."

"Who's Red Eye?" Ranger asked. I could feel all the muscles along my back tense, and I had to force them to relax. Fuck him. He's dead. I won.

Virgil was eyeing both of us. "Meg, I think we're done here. Ranger, I believe we've been remiss in informing you of relevant events. If you'll give me a moment to examine this thing you've brought in, I'll get you up to speed."

Ranger jerked his head, and I took the opportunity to escape out the door.

Greg was waiting for me, and he wrapped an arm around my waist. "Ready?"

"Yup."

"Roof or street?"

"Which route do you want to take?"

He chuckled, leading me over to the stairwell instead of the elevator. "The roof. But you knew that."

"If we don't want to attract attention, I feel like walking would be the answer."

He paused. "Do you want to walk?"

"All the way to the park? Hell no, that's a long ass walk."

We headed up to the roof. Greg locked the door behind us. Yes, he had to use a real key; this building isn't fancy, no keycards. Virgil had actually had to get ahold of and make a copy of the key for us to use. Since we're trying not to garner attention as to where we're living, we couldn't just ask the super for a copy. Greg scooped me up and took off.

He landed in the center of a copse of trees in Ford Harris Park. I mean, it should be safe, no Rat King this time. He took a minute to brush my hair out of my face. I really should put it up if I'm going to be taking advantage of this frequent flyer program so often. The wind from the passage snaps it around so much. When he was done, he left his hand on my face, thumb brushing my cheek.

"I love you," he said.

"I know," I smiled at him. He was smiling too because every time he says that my heart speeds up still. We stared at each other for a long moment. "I thought we were getting tacos?"

"Oh, yeah. Tacos," he seemed to snap out of thought. "They're somewhere around here."

"Going on a taco hunt—" I half sang, pulling him out of the trees with me.

He chuckled. "Please tell me you're not watching kids' songs on YouTube or something."

"Absolutely not." Don't ask me how, the YouTube video spiral somehow sucked me into *Going on a Bear Hunt* and now it's stuck in my head. What? It's catchy. Don't judge me.

He pulled me back against him and kissed me. I gave him a minute before I pulled back. "Tacos," I said sternly.

"Tacos," he agreed.

We set off again, wandering down the paved pathways. There was a very good chance we would never find the taco truck from where we were because Greg had landed us nowhere near where the food trucks are allowed to park, and I had never been to this section of the park before, so I wasn't sure how to orient myself.

Greg's fingers were interlaced with mine, and the path he led us down was surrounded by flowers, bushes, and trees. I could hear a fountain somewhere.

"Where exactly are we?" I asked him. "Because I don't see a taco truck."

"The botanical gardens."

That section was literally *all* the way across the park from where the food trucks were allowed, and this park was huge. I smirked at him. "Decided you wanted to walk?"

"I thought we could spend some time wandering around first, yes. We don't get much time together."

"Hmm, I think we spend a lot of time together," I said because we were almost constantly in each other's orbit.

"I meant quiet time together. Most of the time we're together, Virgil's there, Ranger's there, or we're running around catching bank robbers and jewelry thieves."

"Or running into burning buildings, pulling cars out of the water—"

"Ripping zombie rats apart—"

"Those things were nasty."

"Hmm," he said. "I would like if we could have a conversation that we could keep steered away from hero work."

We had found the fountain. It was surrounded by a riot of color in the flower beds. And no, I can't tell you what kind, the most I can tell is they were pretty. Red - yes, I know I hate red, shut up for a second - yellow, white, blue, purple, pink, even some black flowers. White benches up against the edges of the paved circle surrounded the cascading water. Greg pulled me over to a bench, and we sat down. He wrapped an arm around my shoulders pulling me against him and kissed my head.

We sat in silence, the only noise the rushing of the water. I could smell the chlorine they use to keep the water in the fountain clean mixed in with the scent of the flowers in the air.

"I thought you wanted to talk?" I said after a while.

"Just enjoying the moment. It's quiet here."

"That is not quiet," I said, indicating the fountain because water moving like that is loud.

"I meant quiet *because* of the water. It helps block out all the background noise and I can just sit with you."

"How do you do it?"

"Do what?"

"Sift through all that. How does it not drive you crazy constantly having conversations you're not a part of in your ear? I mean, people chewing must be the absolute worst. You can't tell me you don't hear that."

He chuckled. "You learn to ignore things. If I let every little sound get on my nerves, I'd have to be in a padded and soundproofed room."

"Yeah, if they could even keep you in there."

He chuckled again. He was rubbing one hand on his jeans, but he kept pulling it back so it would hover by his pocket. "Meg," he said, and I leaned into him and kissed him. "Meg," he repeated, his lips against mine. My heart was fluttering, so I hopped up, pulling his hand with me.

"I'm hungry, and I was promised tacos."

'Meg," he said. His fingers caught me, woven in mine so that my choice was to turn back to face him, me standing, him still sitting on the bench.

"Keep saying my name and you're going to wear it out."

He was smiling at me, a glint of amusement in his eyes. I could see his fingers reaching for his pocket; he was shifting toward the edge of the bench. My mouth was dry, my heart pounding.

There was a BOOM in the air.

Greg surged forward, pulling me down, his body wrapped over me so that I was shielded, kneeling on the ground, my head under his chest. I could feel him shift over me, so I turned my head, trying to see what he was doing.

"Meg, wait," he said. I stilled, hesitating. After an eternity of silence, I couldn't stand it anymore.

"What?" I hissed. "What was it?"

"Sonic boom," he said. "I don't know if it's a jet or..." He was shifting again, tense where he pressed against me.

"Oh," I said. You would think I would've recognized the sound. I hear it often enough around Greg when he takes off in a hurry. "Can we get up yet? Because my legs are falling asleep."

"Sorry," he said, getting off me and then helping me up. I rubbed at my thighs; pins and needles are the worst.

Well, whatever moment Greg was trying for was ruined, and I was going to pretend I hadn't had any suspicions. "So, tacos?"

He was looking at the sky above us, squinting, but at my words he looked back down and sighed. "Yeah, tacos."

We headed out of the fountain and flowers grotto side by side, hands in pockets. We were being silent again, meandering back down the path.

"You know," I said, "we can still talk non-hero stuff while we're walking. Just saying."

He smiled at me, but it was distant. I knew that look; he was brooding, and I didn't know if it was over the ruined moment or because he can't help the hero mode. I sighed.

"You want to talk about the boom, don't you?" He didn't answer me, so I pressed on. "You think it's someone else who can fly, don't you?" Again, no answer, so I stopped, forcing him to either walk on without me or halt. He chose to stop, turning to look down at me. "You know I'm just going to badger you until you spit it out, right?"

His lips twitched. "Yes."

"Well?"

"Yes, I think it's someone else who can fly," he said. I stood there with him, waiting for him to elaborate. "Okay, fine, I don't know anyone other than my dad and me who can fly. It's not me, so it's either him or someone we don't know about."

"You worried it's a villain?"

"Little bit," he admitted. "If it's a villain, they can wreak a lot of havoc in a lot of places in a very short period of time, and they're going to be harder for me to track down." We were walking again, still headed across the park, passing by manicured lawns full of people sunning, playing frisbee golf, and various games of catch.

"Which would you rather it be?"

He scrubbed at his face. "What kind of question is that?"

"An honest one?" Because I think I would rather deal with a villain than my parents.

"Villains kill people Meg."

He had poked a sore spot, unwittingly perhaps, and maybe I was also jealous, that things could be so clear cut for him, so easy to decide. "Yeah?" I said bitterly. "So do I. I'm not going to pretend that I'm not going to have a selfish moment of preferring to deal with that over him causing you more pain."

I might be a little sensitive over people who abandon their children.

"You kill bad people." He was choosing to skirt around.

"I still kill people," I snapped. Because I had, and I would continue to do so. The whispers and I could choose nothing else. Vengeance in more than just name, it was all they knew. For a moment, he just gaped at me, surprise and confusion on his face.

"Not like that! You can't, you don't—" he seemed to be

struggling for the words. "I can't let my personal feelings get in the way of what's right."

"Well excuse me for being for human," I snarked, "and sometimes choosing to pick the selfish option."

"I didn't say I didn't want to pick it! I said—"

"I know what you said! So good for you; you're a better person than I am. Because I would choose you over nameless strangers."

He stared at me. He understood protection; he understood being the Fortress everyone sheltered under.

He couldn't understand being Vengeance. It's not always avenging the innocents; vengeance is in the petty, the selfish, the jealous. It's in the rage and fury that comes from being side-lined, abandoned, disregarded. It sounds like it should be associated with justice, but they're nothing alike. Often, you'll find vengeance in the small things, the ones that seem inconsequential.

I spun on my heel and stormed off down the path.

"Meg! Meg, wait!"

If he was anyone else, he would've just caught me. But he's a hero, so he hesitated long enough for me to round a corner and disappear from view. Then I changed direction, striding out onto the lawn, because there were other heartbeats there and it would make it harder for him to find me on sound alone.

If I had been paying attention, maybe I would've noticed him before he grabbed my arm.

"Megaera," he said, his voice as harsh as it had been in the coffee shop. I turned, the whispers in my ears, the figures swirling and curling around my shoulders, shadows pooled at my feet.

"What the fuck do you want?" I snarled at him.

"You found the battlefield," he said, the steel still in his gaze.

"I don't do riddles. If you'll excuse me, I'm busy." Busy getting into a fight with my boyfriend. So not, anything life-threatening or important. I yanked my arm out of his grip and stepped away from him.

I was getting really tired of constantly having to defend my personal space.

He followed me, and the whispers seemed recalcitrant. They didn't want to engage with him, so that left me the option of either turning back toward Greg to get rid of my new follower or hoping I could shake him off. Or I could stand right here, in a space full of witnesses.

No one ever said I always choose the smart option. In fact, I think I've pretty well proven I often choose the stupid one.

I continued across the lawn, the whispers, the figures and the shadows flowing along with me, people looking up and backing away, unable to see what was there, but they could sense it, the unease spreading through the air. I was headed for the trees on the other side. If Greg was looking for me, all he would have to do was follow the path I had just cleared.

"Megaera," my follower said insistently.

"No one calls me that," I said. I paused, halfway across the lawns, trying to determine where I was, and how close the area I was heading to was to the city streets. Now I had a clear circle around us, except for this asshole.

"I call you that. Don't you remember?"

"Remember what?" I snapped.

He regarded me coolly for a moment. "You'll have to excuse me; my answers will be slow. I'm still adjusting to this body and this age's way of speaking."

"Okay, we're done here. Now you're getting too weird for me." I am just not into starring in an episode of *Invasion of The Body Snatchers*, thank you very much. I started walking towards the trees again, more people clearing out of my way.

"How long have you been in this body?" he demanded, his voice taking on an edge of concern.

"I don't know what kind of alien you think I am, but we don't ask that question here."

This time he grabbed me by both upper arms, jerking me around to face him. "How long, Megaera?!"

The whispers howled, and the figures unfurled, rushing forward and circling up his arms, shadows darkening the ground. He dropped my arms and backed off. They flowed back to me, sharks in the water again as they swirled around me.

He looked unsettled, but he was unharmed, untouched by either the fear or the fury. They hadn't tried to hurt him. Or they couldn't.

I needed to get away before he realized that.

I darted back the way I had come, back toward Greg. "Megaera!"

He was chasing after me; I could hear his footsteps behind me. Fuck, he was fast. I leapt over the bushes, caught my foot, tumbled, rolled, and popped up. I'll never bitch at Virgil for making me practice that shit for training ever again. I bolted down the path back toward where I had left Greg.

I heard the moment his feet hit the path behind me.

I took a running leap into the trees at the side. If he was fast enough to keep up with me on flat clear surfaces, let's see if he could handle the undergrowth.

Ford Harris Park is a nice mix of well-manicured and wild, and this section near the fountain grotto was one of the areas they had left to tend to itself, which meant lots of hiding places. I dashed between the trees, surging over the roots, weaving further in, until I found what I was looking for. I slid in, squirming my way back into the center of a cluster of blackberry bushes and ignoring the way the thorns scored deep scratches in my skin, tearing at my shirt and jeans, catching at my hair.

Once I was in a clear space, surrounded by branches, leaves and blackberries creating a canopy and shield, I stopped moving. I stayed down, pressed against the ground, keeping my breath slow and steady. Even though my lungs were burning and demanding air, I kept to the count. Gasping for air was going to give me away. I was going to need to start running religiously if I was going to have to keep these kind of foot chases going. I was out of practice because we hadn't found a good spot to keep up the training Virgil had insisted on at the compound. We couldn't use the parks or city streets for tag.

Footsteps in the undergrowth.

I didn't move, couldn't twitch so much as a muscle. If I made any sort of noise, he would find me.

If I was lucky, Greg could hear my heart pounding and would realize I was distressed, not angry.

The footsteps moved past my hiding spot, but they were moving slowly, shifting around. My back was itching, and I desperately wanted to move branches so I could see exactly where he was.

"Looking for something?" Greg's voice, and I had to fight not to scramble out from cover.

Then the gravelly voice, cool and stoic. "I was. It seems that I'll have to wait for it to be ready to look for me. When it is so inclined, it can find me on the battlefield."

Footsteps crunched in the undergrowth, fading. They were out of my earshot quickly, but Greg hadn't moved, and I wasn't moving until he thought the man was far enough away. Finally, I heard Greg shifting, crouching next to the bushes. He reached in, pushing the branches up and out of the way so he had a clear tunnel he could see me through.

"Hi," I said.

"Hi. What happened? Are you alright? And who was that?" He reached in with his free arm, grabbed my arm and helped me slide back out.

"I'm fine. Just some riddle-laden creep." It was a half lie, and he heard it.

"Why didn't you just make him run? Please tell me you didn't just refuse to use your powers because of me." I could hear the worry in his voice, the concern that our argument had made me act recklessly, that he had said something to make me act that way. That I might have done it to spite him.

"No! He - they - wouldn't."

"They wouldn't? What does that—"

"I don't know! They wouldn't, or couldn't, I don't know!"

Greg scooped me up into his arms. "We're leaving. We'll discuss it with Virgil. I'm getting you somewhere safe." He took us into the air.

CHAPTER THREE

We landed on the roof, but Greg didn't put me down. I squirmed against him. "Why are we-?"

His arms tightened against me. "I'm sorry."

"For what?"

"I forget that you didn't choose this."

"I think I kind of did," I told him. But it was nice he chose to be introspective while we were blasting through the air. I sure hope he paid attention to where we were going.

He snorted, his nose in my hair. He better not have just gotten boogers in my curls. "I feel like you kind of got shoved into it."

"However I got here, I'm choosing to stay."

"But if it comes down to saving the world or saving me—"

"I'm saving you."

He sighed. "We don't get to choose that luxury, Meg. What will Vengeance do if there's no one here to avenge?" There was a different kind of tenseness to him than usual.

I shrugged. "Avenge myself." He chuckled; it was wistful. I raised my face off his chest so I could look him in the eye. "The question is, what would *you* choose?"

"I would want to choose you." I could hear it in his voice, the fear that he would have to choose between saving me and saving innocents. He had already almost lost me once, and it was to something small and mundane.

You can't tell me a Rat King who has to shoot the hero isn't mundane. Come on, how pathetic is that? Okay, maybe it was good contingency planning. Not the point.

But no wonder he was having to fight himself so hard not to lock me up like a porcelain doll, constantly caught between protecting me and saving the world. If I left so he didn't have to choose between the two, would he get over me? Would I get over him? But I'm nothing if not selfish, and I wouldn't take that path because what I wanted was to stay. Heartbreak isn't my style.

I rose up and kissed him because he had given me the answer I wanted to hear. Even if the hero in him made him choose the path that would leave him devastated, I knew which path he wanted, and that was the part that mattered to me.

He had a hand in my hair, his other skimming along my back, fingers warm where they brushed my skin. I slid my hands up his chest, twining my arms around his neck, pressing in against him. "Meg," he murmured against my lips, "we're supposed to be reporting to Virgil, and I'm not doing this on the roof in full view of the office buildings."

"Then why is your hand in my shirt?"

He pulled his hand away, cleared his throat. "Habit."

I laughed. He smiled sheepishly at me. His fingers slid down my arm to my hand, and he stepped away, pulling me with him. "Come on, Virgil first, then we can go hide in our apartment."

I sighed and followed him inside and down the stairs.

Virgil stepped out of the lab into the hallway. He must have seen us come back on the monitors. He stopped in the doorway, his eyes flicking down to my free hand and then back up to our faces. "You're back sooner than expected. Was the taco truck not there?"

"We didn't make it to the food truck," Greg said. "There was — an incident."

"Who'd you have to take out?"

"That's just it, we didn't. Meg says the whispers wouldn't or couldn't."

"Lab, now." He didn't wait on us, just turned and went back in. Greg and I followed him, one of Greg's hands on the small of my back. He was steering me again.

Once we were in the lab, Virgil pointed at a stool all the way across the room. "Sit."

I rolled my eyes but went over to the stool. "I'm not a dog, you know. You could say please."

"Please have a seat, Meg."

"Since you asked so nicely," I said. I settled on the stool, feet in the rungs.

Virgil settled himself on another stool, leaning forward on his elbows, hands steepled. "Explain, and start with the meeting between you and this person. Not the part where you had to use your powers."

"Well then technically it started at the coffee shop—"

"I thought you said it was Maniac at the coffee shop?" Virgil asked, a sharp glance at Greg.

"It was—"

I interrupted them. "You telling this story or am I?"

Virgil returned his gaze to me. "Yes, you were. Continue please."

"I went to the coffee shop, and this weirdo got in line behind me calling me Megaera and claiming he knew me. Then he tried to get me to leave with him, and *that's* when Maniac came in. It looked like he didn't want to try and take both of us on, so he left and told me to find him on the battlefield."

"That's what he said at the park," Greg said.

"I'm not done. Anyway, Greg and I got separated at the park, and I ended up on the lawns—"

"How and why did you get separated?" Virgil asked. Greg cleared his throat, rubbing the back of his neck. Virgil watched him for a moment. "I see. Unimportant to the overall story, I assume?"

"Yes. Well, Greg's dad might be in town—"

Greg was making a slashing movement over his throat, but it was too late. Virgil had already heard.

"Hmm. Greg, stop that. One thing at a time. Meg?"

"Anyway, I was on the lawns, and this same guy was there, and he told me I had found the battlefield. I didn't have time for dealing with some random weirdo and his shit, so I kept trying to get away, except he kept following me, and he kept asking me how long I had been in this body. He grabbed me, and the figures went after him, but they didn't *do* anything to do him. He let go of me at least. I ran because I didn't want him to realize they hadn't tried to or couldn't hurt him."

"And?" Virgil prompted.

"Oh, I hid in a blackberry bush, and then Greg showed up and scared him off. Before he left, he said the same thing about the battlefield."

Virgil sat there watching me. I hate when he does that because it means he's thinking, and he's going to ask me to do more testing or something. "Have you tried asking the whispers why they didn't hurt him?"

I opened my mouth to retort but had to close it because I hadn't. I had only paid attention to the fact that they were reluctant in the first place, and then when they didn't do anything to him, I had run rather than spend time talking to them.

Hey, it was a reasonable reaction. Dude had just grabbed a hold of me. Run away and live to fight another day, duh. I suppose I could have asked them while I was hiding in the bushes, though.

"Could you ask them now?" Virgil said.

I nodded and closed my eyes, calling to them. Yes, sometimes closing my eyes helps. Also, when I've done this kind of communicating with them, Ranger says my eyes go black and it's creepy. Like, the whole thing, not just the iris. So that's new. Virgil thinks it's linked to the whole "got shot and died" thing, and he might be right. I'm still having dreams of the olive grove, but now fragments of memories are popping up while I'm awake, too. I haven't mentioned that part to Virgil, but I think his theory that my temporary death strengthened my connection to my power is definitely right because instead of a vague sense of emotion and one word answers they give me full sentences now.

They came, sighing in my ears. I asked them, why didn't they hit him? They furled around me, rushing, before answering. *We know him.* Then who is he? *We can't remember. But we know him.* They were frustrated because they wanted to tell me.

I told Virgil what they were saying, the feel of their words pressing against me.

He sat silently for a moment. "If they can't tell you who he *is*, can they show you what they *do* remember?"

"Like, images?"

"Yes."

I shrugged. "I'll try." I did, asking them to show me what they knew. Then we were there, a battlefield so strong in my mind it was like I was standing there. Bodies were strewn over the ground, and the dirt was slick with blood - human and horse - abandoned shields, a broken chariot; smoke was thick in the air from pyres that had been set up to one side. Carrion birds were calling overhead. Whatever had happened here was over. His gravelly voice sounded to one side of me. "Glorious," was all he said.

Then the image changed: a dark tent lit only by a brazier. A bed piled high with furs and fabrics. In a word, sumptuous. The feel of skin sliding on skin, and the voice again. "Megaera, my glorious—"

I jerked away, and the whispers surged off my shoulders, eddying in the air, before they settled against me again.

Oh, fuck no, I had enough problems discouraging Ranger. The whispers were agitated, reassuring: *he won't interfere* they were trying to tell me. *A relationship of* - they were trying to pull the word forward - *convenience?*

Well, that would explain why they wouldn't attack him. Except now my face was incredibly red because *I* had most definitely not had a relationship with whoever that was.

"Meg?" Virgil's voice. I could hear Greg shifting, and I knew he had heard the change in my heartbeat.

I cleared my throat. "They showed me a battlefield, but the battle was over. And a tent. They uh, definitely knew him."

Greg's voice. "They *knew* him?"

"Yes *they*," I snapped. "I sure as shit don't, and not in the way they're telling me."

"When?" Virgil asked.

"When what?" I asked confused.

"When was the battle? What kind of clothing? Weapons?"

"Chariots, um, horses. Shields. Ancient?"

Virgil was silent for another long moment. "I think we may need to seriously consider that your power isn't yours at all."

The whispers swirled, agitated. I opened my eyes. "Excuse me?"

"What I mean is that your power is literally the Furies."

I stared at Virgil, the whispers curling around me. "I'm sorry, what?"

"Well, the other choice is past lives, but you told us: they're coming. Now we have a relative stranger coming in and telling you he'll meet you on the battlefield, asking strange questions and saying he knows you. I think we need to seriously consider that the stories about the gods are not just because they're people with powers, but actual gods."

"That's insane."

"I don't think it is. Your power is the only one we've come across where it talks to you. It makes independent decisions from you. It actively works to protect you when you can't protect yourself. You can give it direction, and it listens when it wants to. It calls you its "anchor." I think you're two separate entities in the same body at the very least."

The whispers were trilling, a sound of triumph. Fingers brushing my face. *Find him*, they told me. I let them go.

"They want me to find him," I grudgingly told Virgil. If I didn't tell him they would just keep whispering it in my ears until I did it.

They're not always on board with the "don't tell Virgil" train.

Virgil nodded. "Then let's find him."

"Excuse me?" Greg said.

"We're going to find him," Virgil said calmly, like that was all there was to it.

"I don't know that—"

"And I don't think that we can just leave him wandering out there with valuable information. He knows something we don't. He has answers Meg needs, and he may have answers we need. If we have a god of old showing up in a city park calling it a battlefield, what do you think that means?"

Greg was hesitating. I knew that look on his face. He was silent for a long moment, his eyes on mine. "Okay."

"Okay," Virgil said, clapping his hands together. "I'll get a hold of Ranger. When we do go down to find this god, I think we should go down in force. Just because he's been *friendly* with the Furies doesn't mean he's a friend to the rest of us. In the meantime, you two should probably eat something since the taco truck was absent." He watched us for a moment. "Shoo."

I hopped off the stool and headed for our apartment, and Greg followed me. He shut and locked the door behind us. We stood there, my arms wrapped around myself, space left between us that normally wouldn't be there.

"Are you okay with this?" he asked me.

"Are you?" I asked. Because I wasn't entirely. Just because I, personally, wasn't the one who had a god as an ex didn't meant Greg wouldn't view it that way. The whole thing made me distinctly uncomfortable, coming from first person view as it had.

"Meg—" he sighed, stepping up behind me and wrapping his arms around me so now I was trapped by both my arms and his. "Whatever came before us, I don't care. What matters is now: our relationship, what happens between us. Not whatever happened between him and them."

"Why are you always so reasonable?" I muttered.

"Oh, you're going to argue with me over not being mad at you? Because I think your assessment is inaccurate."

I twisted my head to look at him. "Are you doubting me?"

He chuckled. "That depends."

He loosened his arms enough that I could turn to face him, and I let my arms drop so I could step closer, and I did, pressing myself against him. "I'm pretty sure we determined doubting me wasn't allowed."

"I don't recall that being for all things, just one very specific subject."

"Hmm," I said. I slid my hands up the back of his shirt. "I think we should revisit just how many subjects."

"You know, I think we're just going to table that discussion for a time where you're not cheating to win it."

I stuck my tongue out at him. He laughed and swept me up off my feet, his lips on mine. I had to shift my arms from his back to around his neck. He had one arm against the back of my thighs, one hand on the middle of my back. He broke off the kiss, looking me in the eyes. "I love you," he said seriously. "Nothing's going to change that. Not gods, not men, not even the end of the world."

"I know," I told him, and I kissed him, but after a moment he broke it off again to look at me.

"Marry me," he said.

I froze, my heart pounding, a strange soaring sensation in the pit of my stomach, but I couldn't speak.

"Fuck," he said.

"Yes," I said. The word popped out of my mouth before I could think it through.

What did I just say yes to?

"Which – yes to-?"

"Both," I said, before I could stop myself. If I hesitated, if I paused to gauge this leap, I wouldn't have the courage to make it. Because in that moment all that mattered was the question and the answer, and I hoped he could hear that I meant it in the beat of my heart.

"I – what?" he said, hopefully, as if he had heard my answer but hadn't quite processed it.

"Yes, to both," I repeated, my voice thick.

"That's not how I meant to ask you," he said ruefully, but he was smiling at me.

"I don't care," I said. Because it was perfect. A quiet moment between just the two of us. No grand sweeping gestures, no battles, no parks, no romantic overly priced restaurants, and no other people. A serene instant of normalcy in a life filled with villains and monsters.

Tacos are overrated anyway.

∞

He put a ring on my finger: a mid-century engagement ring, a center diamond held in a square of white gold, flanked by two smaller diamonds in triangles of the same metal, with a yellow gold band. Simple, low profile.

"It was my grandmother's," he said.

"Which one?"

"Paternal." That explained why neither of his brothers had laid claim to it for their wives, although based on what kind of rings they had been wearing, this one wasn't their style. The ring was probably lucky Greg's mom hadn't pitched it in the trash at some point. He must have heard something of my thoughts in the beat of my heart or the look on my face because he explained further how it ended up in his hands. "My grandfather gave her this ring when they got engaged. My father never used it; he left before they died. My grandmother left it to me. They had a happy marriage."

Now I had to wonder exactly how long this ring had been hiding in Greg's sock drawer. Although it would explain why he had been so set on getting someone to give him his stuff back when he and the politicians had parted ways. But it was nice to know the ring had positive associations. It was perfect, elegant but understated. It was pretty but wouldn't be an attention grabber.

I'm not into gaudy in case you can't tell.

We did also manage to make it to the bedroom after that moment.

Excuse you, but I think that's enough information. Is your name Tom?

He was propped on one elbow, drawing circles on my back. "Do you want to be there when I tell my mom?"

"Do I have to?"

"Generally, both parties attend this kind of thing, yes."

"Are your brothers going to be invited?"

"No, I'll just call them."

"Hmm, then I'll consider making an appearance. Can we do it in public?"

He chuckled. "I thought you hated that."

"I do, but I'm not sure your mom likes me."

"She likes you. She just doesn't like your job."

"Well, that makes two of you."

He laughed, leaning forward so his breath tickled my ear and neck. "You wouldn't be you if you had a job I liked." He kissed me, lips trailing down to the hollow of my throat, and I shivered. He was sliding his hand lower, fingers brushing along the curve of my spine. I turned my head to catch his lips with mine.

We both heard the knocking at the apartment's front door. Greg threw his hands up. "Jesus Christ." He levered himself up out of bed, snatching his boxers and jeans off the floor. "The fucking timing shit needs to stop." And then he slammed the bedroom door behind him. "Damn it!"

I snorted, giggling. I bet he got the door stuck again. They were going to have to replace the frame when we moved out. I rolled myself out of bed, grabbing clothes out of the drawers.

What? I want clean ones. The other ones were dirty from the chase in the park. Get your mind out of the gutter; they're literally covered in dirt and leaves.

I was pulling on a shirt when Greg came back and popped the door free. "It's Ranger," he said, sounding only mildly less put out than he had a moment ago. "He said he's seeing snakes."

"Where?" I asked, shaking my hair free, and reaching for shoes.

"Back at the museum."

"Same statue?"

"He's not sure."

Which meant whatever was about to go down, I was going to be present for. We had found through trial and error that if Ranger's visions came in clearly, I wasn't going to be where it was when it happened, but if I was involved, things would come in piecemeal. I looked Greg in the face. "Do you want me to stay behind?"

"No," he answered me too quickly.

"Liar," I said, hopping up off the floor. "Does Virgil have that new outfit for me?"

I could see the relief on his face. "Let's go ask." He grabbed his own shirt and shoes before we headed out. Ranger was still waiting at the door, and I saw his eyes flick down to my hand and back up. His lips thinned. He took a step back out of our way, letting Greg lead the way to Virgil's lab just down the hall.

Virgil looked up when we came in, marking his place and setting aside the book he was engrossed in. His eyes also flicked down and up, but he smiled at us. "Finally. But I assume you're here for something else?"

"Is Meg's outfit ready? Ranger's saying he's seeing

snakes."

Virgil got off his chair, strode over to a full-length cabinet, and pulled something out. It looked like a dull black, one-piece, skintight, long-sleeved jumpsuit. "Yes."

I stared at it. "What is that?"

Virgil looked at it, then back at me. "Polythene Fiber. Forty percent stronger than Kevlar, and they can do the weave thinner so it's easier to move in."

"Yeah, no. Give me back the Kevlar; that at least looked like armor. That's – I'm not running around in a fucking catsuit."

I heard Ranger snort behind me.

Virgil sounded exasperated. "This isn't meant to be worn as *the* outfit. I want it under your clothing. I think it would be best if you can't be picked out as a hero on sight."

"You don't think someone is going to notice when I'm wearing long sleeves in eighty-degree heat to cover up the sleeves on that thing?"

"Plenty of people wear long sleeves in all kinds of weather. I don't think you'll stick out that much."

"Fine. Whatever." I held out my hand. "Gimme." Virgil held it out to me, and I grabbed it out of his hand, stalking off back to my apartment to get changed.

I had a problem: I didn't own any long sleeve shirts. I ended up rooting around in our closet and came up with a sweatshirt of Greg's.

Yes, I have a jacket, but I'm not risking it getting ruined. It's nice and one of the few quality pieces I bought myself. I'm going to have to go back out and get some cheap stuff that I won't care if it gets covered in blood.

When I came out of our bedroom Greg was waiting. "That's mine," he said.

"It's comfy," I said.

"Uh huh. If that gets snake guts on it, I'm going to be mad."

"I'll do my best to avoid that." We were heading into

the hallway, where both Ranger and Virgil were waiting. I paused, looking at them. "Are we all going?"

"This snake was bigger than the last ones," Ranger said.

"How much bigger?"

Ranger paused, his head tilted, his eyes taking on that blank look. Then he snapped back. "Bigger than the statue."

"How much bigger?" I demanded. "I'm not looking to be in *Anaconda*. Watching it was bad enough."

Doesn't everyone have an irrational fear of being eaten alive by a giant snake? No? Just me then?

"You know, I think you're safe. You'd be hard to swallow," Ranger sounded amused, which took the sting out of what might have just been an insult.

"Hummer, now, please," Virgil said. "Even if the snake won't eat Meg, if it's showing up now the museum is open, which means it could potentially dine on other people."

"I think it would only be one person," Ranger said.

"One person is one too many," Virgil said, hitting the down button for the elevator. "Greg, would you go ahead of us and start clearing people out?" Greg took off down the hall for the stairs up, without me.

I protested. "Evacuation is my job."

Virgil fixed me with a hard stare. "Are you going to wrestle the snake?" The elevator doors opened, and between Ranger and Virgil I got herded onto it. "Let him operate without the distraction; we'll clear out rooms as we make our way back. Because I sincerely doubt he'll have time to remove them all."

I flared up. "Excuse you, but—"

Virgil overrode me before I could finish. "Yes, excuse me. But considering recent events, I feel giving him time to think of you as safe at the back is in order. Congratulations, by the way."

I glared at Virgil, stuck at the back of the elevator, the two of them between me and the doors. Not that I could go anywhere anyway, since the elevator had already started its descent. "Fine," I muttered, leaning against the wall, arms crossed.

We reached the bottom, the doors sliding open to the garage under the apartment building and both Virgil and Ranger surged forward, headed for the Humvee.

I know what Virgil called it. What it is, is a Humvee, but my steadfast refusal to remember to call it that has all of us calling it a Hummer at this point.

I prowled after them. The doors on the driver's side swung open while we were still several feet from it, and both of them jumped in.

"Meg!" Virgil called. I sped up, springing up onto the running board; Ranger reached out, catching my hand and hauled me in. He had to half climb over the metal hump between the seats to reach me. He backed up out of my way so we could sit down. Virgil didn't wait for us to be ready past that. The doors slammed shut, the engine roared, and we were off.

I got belted while Ranger yelled, "Cars!" A gust of air, and the vehicles barreling toward our side slowed. Virgil swung the Hummer into traffic.

"I could've handled those," he said.

Ranger snorted. "You drive. I'll handle the traffic." He climbed forward so he was in the front passenger seat.

"Seat belt," Virgil told him. Ranger shot him a look but belted himself in.

Maybe the giant snake would've been the safer bet. I'm totally tattling to Greg.

CHAPTER FOUR

The Hummer didn't skid to a stop in front of the museum so much as it came to a sudden and complete halt, rocking on the shocks. The doors swung open, and I scrambled out along with Virgil and Ranger. People were screaming and running down the stairs toward us, and there were a lot. The museum must have been packed today.

Ranger had brought his baseball bat, and he pulled it off the floor of the Hummer and took off ahead of us, dodging around people, narrowly avoiding collisions as he raced up the steps. The only thing saving him from getting run over by all the people was the fact that he was slowing them briefly.

"Damn it," Virgil said. "Meg, behind me, I don't want you getting knocked down." He took off, striding forward, and I stayed as close to his back as I could, following in his wake as he steered people around us so we could have clear space without getting trampled. The crowd was obviously already panicked, and if I used the fear, I could've sent them fleeing back toward the danger.

The doors at the front were shattered, their handles and glass littering the ground. Ranger was nowhere in sight, and the wave of people coming out had slowed to a trickle. Virgil and I went in, the ground and floor crunching beneath our feet. Inside something had slammed down into the main desk, crushing the counter and wood at the front and creating a hole in the circle. Some of the displays from the ceiling had been knocked down, the plesiosaurus hanging precariously from one wire. Sharks were broken and crumbled, strewn over the floor. There were broken bits of walls, and the doorframe leading to the dinosaur exhibit had been smashed. Virgil headed for that door, then he paused turning back toward me.

"Meg, back up; call them. Follow behind me."

I gave him the space he requested and called to the whispers. They were eager; I could hear it in their howls: the way the figures swirled around me, the shadows elongating along the tile of the floor. The figures were scratching at the ceramic.

Virgil went ahead of me, and again, I followed.

The dinosaur exhibit wasn't in much better shape than the entrance, but I had to wonder where the giant snake had originated - in the Greek exhibit? Had it shown up at the front first and that's why the damage was increasing the deeper we went? Where was Ranger?

Wherever it had come from, I could hear the crashing, which meant Greg was engaged with it.

The door that Virgil was headed for exploded; in fact, it took out most of the wall, and Virgil got caught up in it. He went flying along with the wood and plaster and crashed into the triceratops. The space between us was all that saved me from a similar fate.

The snake was in the room, thrashing, its heavy coils slamming into the walls and fossils, scattering bones. They didn't clatter; they crashed, the heavy crack of rock colliding with stone.

If I thought the Rat King had been huge, this thing was enormous. A true monster, it was larger than the brachiosaurus, its gigantic, blunt head brushing the ceiling. Gleaming black eyes gazed at us, the scales at the nose fading from a deep black to a grey as they ran along its thick body. The stomach itself was a creamy golden color.

If I was a reptile-loving person, I would have said it was beautiful.

Greg had his legs wrapped around the base of its head; he was trying to pull its jaw off, but the way it kept rearing back and shaking itself, he couldn't get the grip he needed. The snake was hissing and spitting, weaving in the air as its tail whipped around.

Ranger came dodging around and past me, so that he stepped out of my range, and he had a sword. Or a saber? I mean, it was long, pointy and sharp. That's what matters, right? He bellowed. "CATCH!" hauling it back like a javelin and throwing it straight at Greg. The snake moved. "Fuck," Ranger said, the air twisting, the sword frozen in mid-flight. The snake flung its head back into the sword's path, and as it unfroze, Greg reached out and caught it. He thrust it into the thing's neck.

The snake shrieked. Greg was sawing the sword straight through, toward the spine.

Its heavy coils were slithering; it had spotted Ranger and me, and that thing was fast and pissed. Ranger was dodging back toward me. "Meg! Send them back! I can't keep it off you if they're—"

But they weren't listening, because like sharks they could smell the blood and they had spun forward, swaying with the snake as they sank their fingers into it, carving gaping wounds up its soft underbelly. It reared away, but they clung to it, a feeding frenzy free for all.

The triceratops bones clattered forward, and Virgil climbed out of them, his face streaked with blood. He waved a hand, and the back half of the snake shuddered to a stop. The top half had Greg on it, and Virgil couldn't hold the whole thing without affecting Greg.

The sword burst free, and the snake collapsed, its body twitching, fangs still snapping, head half-attached. Greg shoved his way out from under the snake, staggered to his feet, and punched it. "Fucking stay down." He was panting.

"Tell it how you really feel," Ranger said.

The figures were still tearing into it, and Greg staggered away.

The whispers were screaming, and I was trying to catch the words, but they were jumbled, too many at once, like the din of a crowded restaurant.

"Meg, you can pull them off. It's dead," Virgil called from across the room.

Ranger was in front of me because he was the only one who could get past the fear the whispers were putting into the air. "Meg, Meg!" I waved him off.

"Wait, they're—" it finally came through. "Cut it open! Someone's in it!"

"Pull them back!" The figures flowed away, and Virgil raced forward, his hands hovering over the body, "Here! Cut it here!"

Greg snatched the sword back up, slicing down the belly. The entrails sagged forward, free of the muscle. Greg dropped the sword and ripped into the stomach with his hands. It tore apart, and a body slid out.

It was the cashier Ranger and I had gotten our tickets from. Eyes sightless, fixed, her face was purple, tongue swollen and protruding. Ranger ran forward, pausing over her. "Fuck," he said, "too late."

The three of them stood there, a tableau in the same pose: fists clenched, heads hanging, shoulders slumped, balanced in their grief.

Uncertain, I hung back. I had been thinking of those nameless strangers as abstract. Faced with someone real, a person I had spoken to, I realized I wasn't used to this feeling of being too late to save someone, but the whispers were, and they sighed in my ears. The sound of it filled me, curling through my veins with every beat of my heart. And we agreed on one thing: vengeance. We would find the one behind the giant snake, whether it was god or man, and we would make them pay.

The figures gathered against me, the whispers curling in the air, shadows rising, flowing forward with me. We went, leaving the heroes to their sorrow. There was work to do, and the man from the park could tell us what was going on.

∞

Was it serendipity or something else that the park was located directly across from the museum? Not the lawns, no; to reach the battlefield he had spoken of, I would have to cross the entire length, a space of more than 50 blocks in length.

The whispers and I were in for a long walk. Relentlessly, we went, flowing forward, my feet as quick as they were. As they eddied through the air, they urged me onward, shadows pouring over the path as the people in the park fled from us. The figures cleared the way as we made the long journey, past the food trucks and the zoo, where the animals in cages roared, howled and screeched as we moved by. They had no way to run from our approach.

We were flying along because it wouldn't be long before they realized we were gone and Greg came looking for us. The figures were slithering through the air, the whispers curled around me, as we raced onward, ever onward.

When he came into view, we slowed. We were at the top of the hill leading down the high ground. He turned and watched us, a salute the acknowledgement of our advantage.

He gestured to his side. He had set up a picnic. Inwardly I scoffed, and the whispers jeered with me, but still, we went to him. When we stood only feet from him, he finally spoke.

"Megaera—" his voice as harsh as ever.

"No one calls me that." I said, and the whispers echoed me.

"What do the people of this age call you?"

"Meg."

"Meg, you are as glorious as you ever were."

This time I echoed the whispers. "Compliments and flowers don't suit you."

"I've missed you," he said reaching for me, and the whispers and I withdrew. He dropped his arm.

"That doesn't suit you either," we said.

"So you do remember?" he asked, cautious.

"No," we said. "Who are you to us?"

"War," he said simply. It was all the detail we needed to know his name.

The whispers sneered. "You were more than that."

He turned to look at the picnic. "Destruction," he admitted, "and more." And then, almost as if it was an afterthought, "The mortals got so many details of our stories wrong."

"We often get the details of our own stories wrong," I told him.

He smiled at me, but it was tight, the kind that doesn't reach the eyes, disingenuous. "So you do. How long have you been in this body?"

"Since the first beat of the heart," the whispers and I said.

"Ah," he said sadly. "No wonder. You always were reckless."

"I like to think I'm just cautious enough."

"Huh," he said, his attention caught by something behind me. "It would appear your guardian—" a pause and he corrected himself, "—guardians have found you."

"Maybe I'm their guardian."

"It would be like you. You always were impossible."

"I hear that a lot."

Ranger stepped up next to me, and I turned my head to look at him. He had his baseball bat propped against his shoulder. "Who's your friend, Meg?"

"Ares," I said. "What happened to the sword?"

"Left it behind. Civil war relic. Don't really want to hold onto something like that. Bat's better for bludgeoning anyway."

"Hmm," I said. Ares was watching us.

"Meg—" Virgil was calling, "could you?"

"Oh, right." The whispers went; I had done what they wanted, and they were willing to wait in the ether.

"Who's your friend, Meg?" Virgil said.

I snorted.

Ares looked irritated. "Do they just all repeat each other?"

Greg stepped up next to me. "No, we don't, because I don't care who you are."

Ares eyed him, taking in his stance. "Ah. I can see why. Interesting company you've chosen to keep."

I shrugged. "I'm capricious."

"You are that," Ares agreed.

"You sure say I'm a lot of things."

Virgil cleared his throat. "I do believe introductions are still in order."

"Right. Guys, this is Ares."

"*The* Ares?" Virgil asked sharply.

"Yes, *the* Ares."

"For those of us who don't know who that is-?" Ranger said.

"God of War," I said.

"Wait, seriously?"

Ares raised an eyebrow at me. "As charming as this discussion is, aren't you going to tell me who they are?"

"I was getting to that," I wasn't. I pointed. "Ranger, Vigilante, Fortress." I wasn't sure why I felt the need to use Virgil and Greg's pseudonyms, but I did, keeping who they are close to my chest.

"So, now what?" Ranger asked.

Ares motioned at the picnic. "We talk. Meg and I have much to discuss, and it would appear that I will have to include you. If I remember nothing else about her, it is that you can't make her do anything."

"That sounds like the Meg I know," Virgil said.

"If you're all going to gang up on me, I'm out," I said.

"Sit," Ares said. "I would offer you refreshments, but I had not planned for quite so many people."

"We're not hungry," Greg said, the challenge in his voice clear.

Ares regarded him coolly, eyes flicking up and down. "I would tell you I approve of this one, but you don't care if you have my approval anyway."

"Nope," I said.

Ares nodded and then moved over to the blanket he had laid on the ground and sat down. Then he waited. No one else moved. I rolled my eyes, stepped forward, and sat across from him. Greg sat on my left, Ranger on my right; Virgil remained standing at my back.

"Ask me your questions," Ares said.

"What the fuck is going on?" I said.

Next to me Ranger snorted, and I could practically feel Virgil wince. Greg set his hand on the small of my back.

"Do you remember anything?" Ares asked.

"Let's just go with no."

"Assume she's as ignorant as to what's going on as we are," Virgil said.

Ares looked up at him. "The gods are returning."

"Yup, got that much," I said. Ranger's lips were twitching.

"Do I amuse you?" Ares asked, fixing that cool stare on Ranger.

"I'm easily entertained," Ranger said.

The look in Ares' eyes hardened.

"He's mine," I said, laying claim to Ranger the only way a god would respect. "And before we get into any further ownership-related issues, they're all mine. Any offense to them is an offense to me." The whispers hissed in my ears in agreement. I could feel Greg's arm trembling against my back and the way Virgil's feet shifted as he fought the urge to run.

Ares relaxed back into his easy-going stance, but I could see the hardness in his eyes that exposed the lie. I should have seen it sooner. He was always ready for battle, as bloodthirsty as ever. He was good at faking the amenable.

"I will ignore the insults, for you," he said. The air around us cleared.

Virgil cleared his throat. "So, the gods are returning. What does that mean for us?"

"A return to the old ways. We will rule the mortal world once again. Some of us miss the worship," he paused. "I do not."

"People never really liked you much," I said. "I don't remember a whole lot of worship going on."

He motioned at the lawns around us. "My worship was in the battles. The mortals still fight their wars. They always will. I have nothing to miss because it never ended."

"How many of you are here so far?" Virgil asked.

"So far, Hera, Bacchus and I."

"Bacchus?" I said, surprise coloring my voice. Did he decide he didn't like Dionysus?

"Yes. He is thrilled with this age's hedonistic ways. He calls it 'clubbing?'"

I couldn't help it; I giggled. "I think he and Ranger will get along. Best friends forever."

"Back on topic, Meg," Virgil said. "How come you remember what you are, but Meg doesn't?"

"It's in how she chose to anchor herself. We don't do that, we don't—" he paused, eyes on me before he refocused on VIrgil, continued on dispassionately. "I can't tell you exactly what happened. We don't anchor ourselves in a child as it forms. We never anchor ourselves in children."

"I wouldn't expect that kind of consideration from a god," Ranger said.

Ares shot him another look. "We don't do it for the child. We don't do it because then we have to wait for that mortal body to grow to be of any real use."

"Who else is coming?" Virgil asked.

"Athena—" Ares tone was sharp and biting, "Aphrodite may; she was undecided last I knew. Hermes, Hades has always been here. He has to stay to gather souls."

"I thought he stayed—"

"No," Ares said. "Your mortal tales speak of a Grim Reaper, and that is Hades. He doesn't stay in the Underworld. He is on the battlefield as often as I am." He rubbed the bridge of his nose. "Poseidon, certainly; he is angry. The seas were his domain, and he doesn't like what you've done to them."

"He a Mother Earther?" I snarked.

"No, the seas are his home. Would you want someone trashing your home? Trespassing in the depths? His anger is purely centered around the fact that he's not the one trashing his own home."

"Anyone else?" Virgil asked.

"Eventually, they will all come," Ares said, "but there is only one who matters."

"Zeus," I said.

"Yes," Ares said, "and he has taken an interest in you beyond what it used to be." He was silent, his jaw set. "I do not like it."

"What kind of interest did he used to have?" Virgil asked. He sounded wary. I couldn't blame him; I was wary of Zeus as well.

"He used to only have an interest in Meg when he was offended but considered it too small for him to punish the party himself. He could be charming and would wheedle her when he was in the right mood. He was one of the few who could get her to follow along with his bidding."

"Probably because he could've crushed me if I didn't," I muttered.

Ares' lips twitched. "Likely. But you would push it and lead him on a merry dance to find just the right way to appeal to you. I think he enjoyed the chase as much as the results."

I could feel Greg tensing next to me, and Ares could see

57

it.

"Not like that," he added. "She and he do not have the history she and I have, which may be why his interest in her has changed. This mortal body entices him."

I could feel my face heat up because I knew what happened to women, god or mortal, that Zeus found attractive, and I'm not down with that. I cleared my throat. "Hera's not gonna be cool with that."

"No. She's not," Ares said, and I could see he thought that was amusing.

"I'm glad this is all a big joke to you," I snapped at him.

"I assure you; it is not."

"Then what are you doing here? You sought me out."

"I'm here to help," he said. "I like this world the way it is. The mortals' ways of killing each other is ever inventive. I do not want the other gods interfering and dragging them back to horses and chariots. How banal it all was." He stood. "I think our discussion is at an end for now."

"No, it's not," I said. Because we still hadn't asked about the snake. "Who the fuck set a basilisk free in the museum?" If the stories about the gods were wrong, the ones about the monsters could be too, and a basilisk was the closest comparison to what we had just killed. As long as it wasn't a Hydra. Please don't be a Hydra.

He furrowed his brow. "The monster that could do that died eons ago."

"Well, I don't think she did because the fifty-foot snake begs to differ."

"He," he corrected. "And Perseus was only the brother of the heroine who killed it. They didn't even get the names right." And he vanished.

We were left sitting in the grass because he had taken the blanket with him. Then all three heroes moved at the same time, Greg and Ranger turning their heads while Virgil loomed over my back, scrutinizing. I could feel my shoulders tense, drawn in.

"So," Virgil said, "I thought we had decided we would meet him in force."

I cleared my throat and stared down at the grass, my face hot and prickling. "Sorry."

"Would you care to explain why you left without speaking to any of us and immediately headed out to meet a god of dubious motives?" Virgil asked.

The whispers could not feel embarrassment or shame like I could. To feel that way was beneath them; we had chosen our path and it was the right one. Had it been anyone else, they would've told him their business was their own.

For me, they would be willing to try for contrition.

"The cashier," I finally told them.

"Ah," Virgil said.

They were silent again, the wound of being too late to save someone still fresh.

Ranger and Greg finally stood, and they both offered me a hand up at the same time. I took both, rising to my feet between them.

Steady on my sea legs, I slid my hand out of Ranger's, but left the other with Greg, whose fingers tightened briefly on mine.

It was in that moment that I became aware of all the people crowding the park.

The whispers and I may have run them off for a while, but once they were gone, and the people had a chance to realize there was nothing to fear but fear itself, they had drifted back in while we sat and talked to Ares. A lot of them were staring at us.

I mean, wouldn't you stare too? One man covered in blood and slime, another dusty, freely bleeding from head wound, the third sporting a baseball bat nowhere near the batting cages? And all three had surrounded a woman wearing an oversized sweatshirt in the summer heat.

Virgil made an irritated noise in his throat. "I need to get my car. The reporters are going to have swarmed the museum by now."

I realized that Ares hadn't technically confirmed that what we had just fought was a basilisk. If it was a Hydra, we had a problem. "Wait, wait, is it really dead?"

"I'm pretty sure it's dead," Greg said.

"But did you check? We have to go back." My voice was going shrill, "We have to—" But Virgil and Ranger had already reacted to the panic in my voice and were racing back toward the museum. Greg pulled me up against him and took off. A dizzying, breathless moment, and he was landing on the museum steps.

Ranger and Virgil were going to be at least ten to fifteen minutes behind us, and that would depend on how quickly they could run the distance.

The news vans were already at the curb, reporters and cameramen unloading. Police stood at the bottom of the stairs with a barrier to keep them back.

Police and EMS had beaten us here, and Greg shoved his way past the officers who had been set to guard the doors, pulling me along in his wake. We dodged around the paramedics who were standing in the lobby. They had no one to save and were waiting for the coroner to come confirm what they already knew.

One of the officers from the door was trying to chase after us, yelling that we couldn't be in here. Pretty sure one of the phrases he used was, "Fucking kids!"

We were back in the dinosaur exhibit, and Greg stopped suddenly enough that I stumbled into him. I bounced back, his hand on my arm the only thing that kept me from falling on my ass. He turned and helped me catch my balance before he let me go.

"Fancy meeting you here," said a voice.

"Detective White," Greg said. "I thought you worked robberies."

"New task force," she said. "Thanks to you and the rats, I got assigned to it." She did not sound happy about it.

I cleared my throat. "Snake," I reminded Greg.

"It looks like it's still dead."

"Burn the neck where it's severed."

"With what?" he asked me. "Do you see anything I can set it on fire with?"

The body twitched, its coils sliding and thumping. I squeaked. "Burn the fucking neck!"

Detective White eyed me. "It's been doing that for a while. We think the body just hasn't realized it's dead."

But the body was still moving, the coils now gathering together. "Get everyone out," I told her.

Greg had seen it too. "Fuck. EVERYONE OUT!" he roared. The other detectives didn't hesitate; they ran. White had turned to stare at the snake as it began to rise. The half-severed head was swinging, and at the spine something was forming, pushing its way forward, splitting as it grew. Greg grabbed her arm, shoving her toward the door. "RUN!" He caught my waist, spinning me around. "You too! Run, damn it!"

I ran, the whispers flowing with me as I went. I had to make sure the building stayed clear and warn Virgil and Ranger when they got here. And find something to burn it with.

The officer from the door and the paramedics were still in the lobby, staring confusedly at the people who had just run by. The whispers and I screamed, and they fled before us, and then we were outside at the doors, the whispers, figures, shadows and I guarding the entrance. The detectives had run into the press and were pushing them back from the barriers.

I panted. What would they have? Road flares? Would those work? They should be hot enough, but would the flame cover enough of the surface quickly enough?

Virgil and Ranger were coming up the steps. "What's happening?" Virgil demanded, steps below me.

"Hydra! We need fire!"

I sensed it in the second before it happened, that impending doom moment where you know something bad is about to transpire, and you're in the way.

What was left of the doors behind me blew outward, the entire entrance of the museum exploding as the Hydra's body slammed through it. Something hit me in the back, and I flew forward, straight through the air before gravity took over and I hit the stairs, tumbling the rest of the way down. I had at least had the sense to tuck my head down, covering it with my arms as best I could.

I came to a rest at the bottom of the stairs, half under one of the wooden barriers. "Ow."

I had that brief mental minute where you can't quite remember how to operate your own limbs. Someone was leaning over me, cherry red hair.

"You need a hand?" Maniac asked me.

I waved an arm in what I hoped was the right direction. "Kill it with fire."

"That is one big ass snake," she said. She pulled me to my feet. "Let's get you up so you don't get squashed." We stood for a moment, staring at the two-headed monstrosity as it wove drunkenly in the air, its mouths snapping at Greg as he dodged it. He punched one, knocking it into the other. It hissed in one long shrieking howl of a sound, made all the worse because it was coming from both of them.

I was looking around, trying to find Ranger and Virgil, but I couldn't be sure where they were. I hoped they hadn't gotten crushed under that thing. I could still see where Greg had sliced it open, the intestines spilling and sliding with each movement of the coils, but that didn't seem to bother the Hydra.

"We need to cut off its heads and burn the necks closed," I told Maniac.

"Cut them off with what?"

"There's swords in the Civil War exhibit," I said helpfully.

"Oh yeah, great, because I'm going to be racing past that thing to get in there." She was rising up on the tips of her toes, looking around. "I could get in through an emergency exit, just blast a door open."

"Let's do that then."

"No, I'll do that. You will stay here and make sure that thing doesn't, I don't know, eat someone."

Jesus Christ, does everyone think the only thing I'm good for is scaring off lookie-loos?

But she had already run off, racing around to the side of the building.

The snake struck, driving Greg into the ground. He was pinned, struggling to keep the jaws open, and it was thrashing, straining to close its mouth around him.

The whispers and I went racing up the stairs, our own wail echoing, the figures surging forward, slashing. They carved long gouges across its snout, up its face, and one eye burst. The figures were swirling, shadows stretched along its side as they tore into its flesh. It reared both heads back, releasing Greg.

But now its focus was on me. The whispers curled around me, and they swayed with it. It reared back and up. The mouths opened, fangs extended.

I am so, so fucked.

But it hesitated just long enough, confused by the fear, and by the time its mind, or minds, cleared enough for it to strike at me, Virgil had brought its heads to a shuddering stop. He was off to my left, out of my range, hands extended.

"Meg! Move! I can't hold it for much longer!"

I darted back down the stairs, and its heads crashed into the spot I had been standing in. It reared up again, hissing and spitting, and chased after me. I switched directions, trying to twist around in a U-turn. If I kept going down, I would lead it straight to the people still in the road.

Greg slammed into it, the heads crashing into the steps directly behind me. I kept going; I had to make sure I was out of range. I darted back up the steps, toward the main body, even as it coiled and slithered. I was trying to make my way around it, head into the museum itself.

Which might not be the best place to be right now.

There was a blast of heat, and I ducked back, flames belching out of what was left of the museum's entrance. They were licking at the snake's body, crawling their way up it, its flesh blackening and peeling back from the muscle and bone.

It screamed, an unearthly noise that made the hairs on the back of my neck rise. Now its attention had been attracted by the person standing in the hole that was left of the front of the building, slithering, trying to change its direction.

Maniac had one hand out, fire streaming from her palm, a human flame thrower. Her other hand held a couple of the sabers, and she tossed them in my direction; they clattered across the stone, sliding to a stop at my feet. She brought that hand up to join the other, and the flames doubled in size.

"I'll take those," Ranger said, snatching the swords up off the ground, and then he was gone, racing back towards the heads that Greg and Virgil were attempting to keep pinned to the steps themselves.

The figures and shadows joined the flames, burrowing into the burnt flesh, pulling it further from the bone, ripping at the exposed organs. They burst out the other side and came back to tear at it again.

The heat was intense, and I was going to need to back up, because I wasn't sure my skin wouldn't blister. I started to pull away, the figures and whispers howling because they didn't want to let go. The distance between us stretched, their rage building, and then they settled, circled, swirling around me.

Ranger had gotten one of the swords to Greg and was slowing the Hydra's movement, Virgil pinning it, the two working in tandem so Greg could hack through its necks. Maniac sent flames licking up the snake, burning through the flesh as the wounds opened further. The first head fell.

The second head screamed again, yanking itself back. Virgil and Ranger stumbled and recovered, but not before Greg had leapt on it. He drove the blade down into its head. The saber broke, the sword still embedded in the thing's skull. It shuddered and fell, it and Greg crashing into the stone. Greg kicked free of it, and Ranger tossed him the other saber.

Have you ever heard the way a guillotine thunks down? The thwack of the blade as it moves through flesh? I mean, I've only heard it in movies, so maybe you've got some personal experience you'd like to share. On second thought, don't. Although maybe the sound of a cleaver into meat would be more accurate. Either way, that was the noise it made as Greg hacked through the second head, Maniac still burning the flesh as the blade sliced its way through.

The flames stopped, the remains of the Hydra smoldering. But this time, it was most definitely dead. Blackened and charred, there was no way it was coming back from that.

"Damn," Maniac said. "What a pain in the ass that was."

Greg dropped the sword, turning a baleful eye on her, then walked away from the smoking remains, stopping at the edge of the figures and shadows. They drew away from him, flowing their way back to me, curling up my legs, brushing their fingers against my hair before they faded. He followed in their wake until he stood in front of me. He pinched a sleeve of his sweatshirt, and I looked down at it. Some of the fabric was burnt through. I looked back up at him.

"At least it's not snake guts?"

His lips twitched. "You owe me a sweatshirt."

I would take that. I was worried he was going to be mad at me for not running farther away.

"Excuse me," Maniac called. "But are we done here? Because I got places to be."

CHAPTER FIVE

Virgil had ignored Greg's tooth grinding to extend Maniac an invitation back to our temporary quarters. There had been at least five to six snakes if not more that had come out of that statue, and if all of them were Hydras, we were in trouble.

And we still needed to find the party responsible because if we didn't get to them soon, there were going to be more snakes or Hydras than we could handle.

All five of us rode back in the Hummer. I think Greg was only in it because he wanted to know what Virgil was saying. Otherwise, he would've just flown the two of us back to the apartments. The whole ride ended up being spent in uncomfortable, awkward silence. Maniac sat hunched in the front passenger seat, and Greg planted himself in the center where there was nowhere to sit, his hand resting on the back of her seat.

I feel like he did it on purpose. Well, okay, maybe it was because he was the only one who would be completely fine without a seatbelt.

Either way, we got back, and we got up to our floor. Virgil went off to make some calls. He wanted to get a hold of more swords because we couldn't rely on every location these snakes showed up at to conveniently contain sabers.

Maniac loitered awkwardly in the hall because Greg

marched the two of us right past her, his hand on the small of my back.

He's lucky I'm waiting to yell at him in private. Because he's gonna have to get over whatever she did in the past. Right now, we need her.

I half turned because I wanted to say something to her but caught Ranger's eye. He jerked his head at me: his signal for "on it."

"So, Maniac, how long you been in the hero business?" he was asking her when Greg steered me into our apartment and slammed the door behind us. I heard the frame crack.

Greg sighed and scrubbed at his face. "Damn it."

"Maybe have fewer snits," I told him.

He opened his mouth, then shut it and moved his hand away from me. He walked stiffly over to the couch and sat down on it, too hard. The wood groaned and the legs on his side gave way. It hit the floor.

"God fucking damn it," he swore.

I knew what was going on. He was having to reconsider his, "villains are always bad, don't throw away useful allies" mantras. Because those two don't always play well together. He hadn't been a fan of when we had to work with Mirage either, but in that case, he hadn't had personal history with him, probably because that had been about five years before we met. The part where Mirage "died but didn't die," not the part where he started stalking me. So that cooperation was probably easier for Greg to reconcile.

I walked over, crouched down on the floor, and put my hands on his knees.

Oh, I'm not being cute or trying to give him the mental boost of having the "high ground" because his head is above mine. It's always above mine. It's because if I sat next to him, he would be able to just get up and walk away. This way he would have to knock me over to move, and he wasn't going to do that.

"You don't have to forgive her," I told him. "You just

have to stomach working with her."

He sat silently, brooding before he spoke. "You taking lessons from Virgil?"

"Maybe," I said cheerfully. "I'm not generally this wise and introspective on my own."

He chuckled, leaning forward to kiss me. "I think you're wiser than you realize."

"Well, that makes one of us."

He laughed, and pulled me up into his lap, settling my back against the arm of the couch, his own arm slung over my shoulders. I settled my head against him.

"Next time, can you stay farther back from the fucking snake?" he said.

"That depends. Is it going to be trying to eat you again?"

He huffed. "Wouldn't matter if it did. If it thinks you're hard to swallow, it doesn't want to know what I would do to its stomach."

I raised my head to face him. "This isn't a joke." I think he realized I was serious from the tone of my voice because his expression changed. He didn't say anything, and so I continued. "Some of these monsters, even being invincible can't save you from what they can do. Medusa, Medusus? Whatever his name actually was, he turned people to stone. We can't bank on you being immune to that."

He was silent again, his eyes locked on mine. "Okay," he said slowly. "I'll watch myself."

"Good," I said. "Because if I have to avenge you, first I'm going to come down to the underworld just to yell at you about it."

"I'm going to need a crash course in mythology because I don't know what any of that means."

"How'd you get through school without learning anything about the classics?" I demanded.

"I might have barely passed a few classes," he said, grinning at me.

His phone rang, and he groaned before he pulled it out and looked at the screen. He sighed. "Hi, Mom," he said. "Yes, that's me, on the news, with the giant snake." He sounded aggravated. I mean, I would be too. The reporters stood there and filmed that? What is wrong with them? How come these idiots never run? Their self-preservation instincts are worse than mine at times.

Greg was still talking. "Yeah, I said I have news. No, not over the phone, I thought dinner—" he was listening. "No, I don't want Tony and Peter there—" His tone was still colored with irritation. "Yes, Meg will be there."

I could feel his muscles tensing against me, the fingers of the hand he had set on my leg flexing. He sighed. "Yeah, fine, I'll ask her, but I think we were hoping to go out. Yes, in public. At a restaurant. No, Mom. Uh huh. Yeah, I'll call you back." He hung up and sighed, leaning around me to set the phone down on the coffee table.

"What's up?" I asked.

"She wants us to come to her house for a family dinner so I can tell them whatever is up all at once."

"Hmm," I said. "You think she knows?"

"Yes," he muttered.

See, aren't things much easier for me not talking to my parents at all?

"Are you okay with that, or did you have your heart set on a public space?" he asked.

"You mean where no one can throw a fit if they don't like what they hear?" I asked.

He chuckled. "You don't know my mom."

I kissed him. "Whatever is easiest for you. I don't care if we fly in, yell 'We're engaged!' at them and leave."

"Don't tempt me."

I grinned at him, moving my head so I could whisper in his ear. "Tempt you with what?" He shivered against me.

"Don't do that," he said, but his hands were tugging at my – okay it's still his, but now it's community property –

sweatshirt, slipping under it and the shirt beneath, pulling them over my head. His hands were running over the polythene suit. "How does this thing come off?"

"That's for me to know—" I started, but he shifted, lifting and moving me so suddenly I was lying back against the cushions, his body pressed down against me.

"And I'm going to find out," he growled playfully in my ear. His hands skimmed down, pulling at my pants, and with one quick, fluid motion he had peeled them off, but I heard the moment the fabric tore.

"Hey! I like that pair!" I said.

"I'll buy you new ones." He was focused on one thing. "Where the fuck is the zipper?!"

I laughed.

"Something funny?" he asked me, his breath tickling against my neck, and it was my turn to shiver.

"Absolutely," I told him.

He found the zipper on the back of the suit, and this time he went slow, pulling it down, peeling the suit off my shoulders, his lips following in its wake. His fingers hooked under the strap of my bra to bring it free along with the suit, his tongue trailing along with it.

I heard fabric somewhere else tear, but I had a hand on Greg's shoulder, the other in his hair as he inexorably moved lower, his fingers whispering over my skin, breath warm against me while he drew the suit off my legs.

And honestly, at that point I didn't care what piece of clothing he had just destroyed.

∞

We ended up agreeing to dinner at his mom's house. Mostly because she wanted everyone invited, and that would mean a large party at a restaurant, which would be extra awkward if people reacted poorly. Greg didn't put it past them to find safety in numbers even out in public.

I couldn't subject the poor wait staff or any other diners to that.

Plus, Greg had already promised the first insulting thing any of his family said we would take off. I set up a 911 code text with Virgil anyway. Oh, I trust Greg, but his patience with his family might extend further than mine. It's for everyone's safety technically.

We arrived early, beating both his brothers and their families there and went in through the side door at the kitchen instead of the front, both my hands in my dress pockets. Yes, I dressed up for the occasion, and yes, that little black dress had pockets. Greg's mother waved at us from in front of the stove. She had a couple pots set up.

"There you are!" she said, grabbing a small spoon out of a drawer and dipping it into one of the pots. "Here, taste this."

"What is it?" Greg asked.

"Alfredo sauce."

Greg took the proffered spoon and offered it to me before he took a taste. You know how most Alfredo sauce you get at restaurants is kind of bland? This was not like that; it was good.

"It's good, Mom," Greg said.

She stirred the sauce with a wooden spoon that had been sitting on a rest by the stove. "Good. Now we just need the pasta. Chicken will be done and ready to rest in a minute."

Where Virgil and Greg tended to be calm and fluid in the kitchen, Greg's mother was full of nervous energy, flighty and quick, and her kitchen was too narrow for this many people in it.

"Go sit," she said. "Everyone should be here in a minute. They better be, or dinner will be spoiled."

"Mom, I - we - were hoping to talk to you before everyone got here."

"I've really got to—" She was interrupted when the side door swung open. "Antony!"

"It's Tony, Ma," Tony corrected her.

"I birthed you, I get to—"

"Call me whatever you want. I know, Ma." Tony squeezed past us. "Brit's still getting the kids out of the car, but she wanted me to go ahead and bring you this." He tried to hand his mom a bottle a of wine.

"No, no. Go put it on the table and open it up." She waved us off. "Go."

Greg sighed and gave my hand a pull. "Come on."

We followed Tony out of the kitchen into the dining room where he rummaged in a sideboard and pulled out a corkscrew. "Meg, wine?"

"No, thank you." Oh, did you forget? I don't drink alcohol or do drugs. That whole cognitive function effect and everything. I would've thought that would've been obvious since I combined the two the first time I had either of them. Soda and coffee are my addictions of choice, thanks.

"Not a drinker, Meg?" Tony asked.

"No," I said.

"Why not? Just not drinking right now?" he asked, his voice sharp. Beside me, I could feel Greg tense.

"Never and because I don't like it," I told him, leaning into Greg, a squeeze of his hand. Tony wasn't going to be able to get to me by making insinuations about my lack of drinking. Bet you I've heard worse insults.

Tony shrugged and turned back to the sideboard, pulling wine glasses out.

We were saved from the awkward silence portion of this encounter by the entrance of Brit, all six of Greg's nieces and nephews, Peter, and his wife Sandra, who had made sure the last time we visited to let me know no one ever calls her Sandy.

I was determined to find an excuse to do it.

Greg's mother was coming through, a platter of sliced chicken breast and a bowl of pasta balanced in her hands. Greg let go of me to grab both from her and set them on the table.

She smiled at him. "Thank you, Greg."

"How come he gets called by his nickname?" Peter

demanded.

"Because he doesn't correct me when I use his given name," their mother said. "Oh! I forgot the garlic bread."

The kids were loudly getting seated, Brit and San*dra* getting them served ahead of everyone.

Greg's mother came back with a breadbasket piled high. "Sit!"

There was mild seat blockage while everyone jumped to obey her.

"So, Greg," Tony said, "giant snakes now?"

"No hero—"

"Talk at the table. We know, Ma. But you said Greg had something important to tell us. Is it about the snake, Greg? It's the snake, right?"

"You were there too, weren't you, Meg?" Sandra asked.

"Yes," I said.

"Do anything useful?" Tony asked.

I stared him down. "Yeah, I knew how to kill it."

"Meg was the brains behind that take down," Greg said.

Tony grunted. "Looked like she spent most of it getting chased."

Greg bumped the table, and the dishes jumped. Everyone stopped what they were doing to stare at it and him. He cleared his throat. "Sorry, hit my hand on it."

There was a new air of tension, but everyone turned back to the food for a moment.

"So, if it's not the snake, what's the news?" Brit asked.

"Meg and I are getting married," Greg said.

"Oh, show us the ring, Meg!" Sandra said. She sounded legitimately excited, so I guess I can let the Sandy thing go.

There was the clatter of cutlery from the head of the table. "Married?" their mother said weakly.

"You get her pregnant?" Tony asked.

"Tony—" Peter said, but Tony waved him off.

"You know they have ways to take care of that, right? Shotgun weddings aren't a thing anymore."

"Tony!" Brit hissed. "That's not—"

"No," said Greg, "and if you can't just be happy for us, don't come to the wedding." He pushed back from the table, one hand on my elbow. "Mom, thanks for dinner. Sorry we can't stay."

He led me back out through the side door. Once we were outside the house, he pulled me into him, his nose in my hair. I wrapped my arms around him.

"Fuck Tony," I said.

Greg laughed, but it sounded pained. The side door opened, and we both turned our heads to look. Greg's mother was in the doorway.

"Congratulations," she said stiffly.

"Thank you," Greg said.

"This isn't what I wanted for you."

"It's what I want," Greg said, his arms tightening against me. I flung my arms around his neck, my face buried in his chest, and he took us into the air.

∞

He did not take us home. I mean, we went downtown and landed on a roof, but it wasn't our roof, and for a moment both of us were content to be still, watching the sun reflect off the windows and listening to traffic below.

But you know me, I have to ruin all the moments. "So, what're we doing?"

He kissed my head. "We didn't eat."

"We did not," I agreed.

"You hungry?"

"Is that a real question?" I teased. "Who's cooking?"

"Not you."

I snorted. "I mean, maybe if you wouldn't hover in the kitchen I might get somewhere."

"And risk you taking a whole finger off this time? No." His hands were on my back, his arms just loose enough for me to step back from him if I needed to. I stayed where I was, head tilted so I could see his face.

"Well, if I'm not cooking, what are we doing for dinner?" I asked him.

"Roof top take out?" he asked.

"From where?"

"There's a great little Indian place down at the street."

"Are you trying to expand my food horizons again?"

"Absolutely. You a fan of spicy?"

"Do chips and salsa count?"

"No."

"Then I don't know."

"Hmm," he said. "Okay, wait here. I'll surprise you." He disappeared over the edge.

I settled down on the concrete of the roof to wait. The whispers curled around my shoulders, figures brushing my hair.

Look, we've got giant snakes and an unknown number of gods roaming around. If I'm by myself, I would be stupid not to have the Furies physically out with me at all times.

It was the right move too because he just showed up out of thin air, next to me, sitting on the roof. I started and jerked away from him. He smiled at me. Black haired, and green eyed he was dressed like a 70s stoner in bell bottoms and a vest with no shirt, leaving his chest and stomach bare. He had a half-full bottle of whiskey and smelled of cigarettes, sweat and sex - not a combination I wanted to be anywhere near. He took a pull from the bottle and offered it to me. I shook my head, scooting further away. I knew who he was; I mean, it would have been hard not to recognize him with the whole "Lord of Debauchery" look he had going on, and I didn't want anything to do with it.

"You always were a stick in the mud," he said.

"Nice to know some things never change," I said. The whispers were unperturbed. But then, Bacchus wasn't interested in causing chaos. He was here to have a good time. "Is this going to be a thing with all of you? You just show up

75

for visits unannounced?"

"Some things never change," he told me; I could hear the laughter in his voice. He pulled a pack of cigarettes out, smacking the box against his palm before pulling one out. He offered the pack to me. Again, I shook my head, scooting farther away. He shrugged, put them up, and began patting his pockets. "Got a light?"

"No."

He took the cigarette out of his mouth, rolling it between his fingers while he watched me. "I don't bite," he said, eerily reminiscent of the first time I met Virgil. He shifted, leaning onto one arm so that he could tilt his body toward mine. I could feel the pull of his power, the charisma he projected, and the sense of desire he was putting into the air.

"Not into that," I told him. The whispers giggled.

"Spoilsport," he said, sitting back.

"My favorite thing to do is spoil it for others," I told him, scooting again, slowly stretching the space between us.

This time he did laugh, throwing his head back; if I had been close enough, I could have counted his teeth. His laugh was loud, braying and infectious.

I could feel my lips twitch, but there was no way I was smiling at him, damn it.

He was wiping at his face, the occasional chuckle still making its way out. "Ah," he said. "I forgot how amusing you could be when you're in the right mood."

"I'm so glad you all remember this huge personal history we have together, but I'm going to need you to go now." Eventually Greg was going to be back up here, and I wanted Bacchus to be gone before that point.

"Do you now?"

"Yup."

"As you wish," he said and vanished.

That was too easy. I started to get up because I was going to expand the whispers out, make sure he was gone, but at that moment Greg came up over the edge, and they vanished.

He landed next to me, holding up the takeout bags.

"So, I got us rajma, eggplant curry dip and some—" he was saying, then tilted his head to the side, his brow furrowed, like he was hearing something just out of earshot, and he was trying to listen in.

I could feel it in the air again: a craving, an aching longing, and I saw the moment Greg's eyes glazed. "Oh, fuck."

He dropped the food, grabbed and pulled me to him. His lips were on mine, on my neck, my shoulders. I was trembling against him, fighting against the compulsion, unable to draw back from his grasp. One of his hands slipped up my skirt, and I gasped.

"Meg," he said, his voice in my ear, a groan so different from the way he always said my name.

Not this way.

"Stop, Greg, STOP!" I screamed it, desperate and scared. I could feel the whispers; if I brought them out, they would clear the air around us, but could they do that quickly enough not to harm Greg at the same time?

He stilled against me, shuddering. "Meg," he said, his voice hoarse. But he was him. He was pulling his hands back, staggering away from me. He sounded horrified, his voice a whisper. "What did I do?"

I couldn't hesitate in this moment. If I dodged around the issue, he would be convinced he had done something irreparable. "We're okay," I told him. "You didn't hurt me." Soft, soothing, hand extended. "Come back to me."

He didn't move. "I didn't - Meg, I'm so sorry, I—" his voice cracked.

"Fine, I'll come to you," I said. I stepped toward him, but he took a stumbling step back. This time I stayed where I was and watched him, thinking, and came to a decision because I wasn't sure I was the one who could reassure him in that moment. "Okay, we need to go tell Virgil."

"What? Tell him what? That I almost raped you?" His hands were in his hair, and he was taking another step back from me, the pitch of his voice rising.

"No, that Bacchus is here." If he left, I didn't know how I was going to help him. Nevermind the fact that I'd be stuck on a roof. All I knew at this instant was that we needed Virgil. Virgil could help.

"Bacchus? What does he—"

"Sex, sex god." I interrupted. Simplest explanation. We did not have time for the finer details. My phone rang. I ignored it; I needed to concentrate on Greg, except then it stopped and started ringing again. I left one hand extended toward Greg, pulling the phone out of the skirt pocket and answering it without checking the caller ID. I didn't dare look away from Greg in this moment; he was hesitating, and I needed him to stay with me. "What?" I snapped into the phone.

"Let me talk to Greg." Virgil's voice. Relief flooded me.

I held the phone out toward Greg. "Virgil wants to talk to you."

He paused, still steps away from me. I stretched the phone out as far as I could.

"Your mortal is incredibly strong-minded," said a voice to my left. "I'm impressed. Not many people could buck the compulsion like that, or so quickly."

"Not now, Bacchus, go fuck off," I snarled. I'm not sure if I called him by name on purpose or by accident, but Greg went from horrified to rage-filled. He launched himself forward and slammed into Bacchus, knocking him down and punched him. I heard the snap; I think Greg broke his jaw. Gods must be somewhat damage-proof, though, because anyone else's face would've been smashed in.

Bacchus howled, a combination of a scream and a shout of laughter, and vanished again, and Greg was left panting, crouched on the concrete. I stayed back where I was, unsure whether I should try approaching him or not. Angry was better than before, right?

My phone started ringing again. Virgil must have hung

up and called back, tired of waiting. I answered it, still watching Greg. "We're having technical difficulties."

"I surmised that," Virgil said. "Put me on speaker." I hit the speaker button.

"You're on," I said. Although he probably knew that.

"Greg," Virgil said, his voice steady. "You need to report back here, and *bring Meg.* Do not under any circumstances leave her on that roof. Oh, and don't forget your food." He hung up.

Seriously? Virgil has to have us bugged somewhere. But Greg and I have checked both our phones, our shoes, various articles of clothing, and we can't find them.

But Greg was getting up, and he was stepping up to me, tense and still shaky. "Meg."

"We're good," I told him again. "I'm fine. You didn't hurt me." I put one hand on his chest. "We're good," I repeated. I stepped into him, the other hand on his hip.

Slowly, he wrapped his arms around me. I moved my arms around his neck. His grip tightened, and then we were in the air.

We forgot the food.

CHAPTER SIX

Virgil met us on the roof. "Which one was it this time?" he demanded.

"Bacchus," I said, Greg had already let go of me, stepping away. Virgil noticed.

"My apartment now, Greg," he said, projecting that commanding air he gets, the order floating in the air.

I started to follow them, but Virgil half turned on the stairs down. "Meg, your apartment."

"But—" I protested, dogging Virgil into the hallway.

"Your apartment," he said, blocking the way into his. Greg had preceded him in. He stared me down, and he knew I was about to argue again. "Let me handle this. If I need to bring you in I will, but right now, he thinks he's a danger to you. Give him space." He stepped back, shut the door in my face and locked it.

I stared at it for moment, then spun on my heel, marched down to our apartment and slammed the door behind me. I wanted to jerk it open and slam it again. The whispers swirled around me; *we should hunt him down* they said. My phone pinged, and I pulled it out, a text from Virgil: "DO NOT LEAVE THIS BUILDING."

How the fuck does he do that?

Fine, we'll do it his way. I set my phone down on the

kitchen counter and stomped off to the bedroom, practically ripping the dress off. I threw it at the wall, where it hit, sliding to a crumpled heap on the floor. I threw my heels at the wall too. They left dents in the drywall.

I was still pissed, and I had run out of things close at hand to throw. I pulled clothes out of the dresser - jeans, tank tops - yanking the drawers open and slamming them shut as I went. I pulled them on, then sat down on the floor and cried, swiping at the tears.

There was a knock at the front door.

I ignored it.

They knocked again.

"GO AWAY!" I bellowed.

I heard the door open then heard a voice, Ranger. "You didn't lock it," he said. I didn't answer him. I heard the door shut, and then footsteps. They stopped at the bedroom door.

"Go away," I said, from the floor, hidden behind the bed.

"Or what?" Ranger said, coming around to my side. He sat down next to me, one leg drawn up, the other stretched out so that his boot was resting against the dresser. "You don't scare me."

I snorted, still swiping at tears.

Ranger pulled one of those little travel packs of tissues out of his jacket and offered them to me. I took them but didn't open it.

"I thought you were entertaining Maniac," I said.

"Virgil asked her to go do recon," he said. "About, twenty, maybe thirty minutes ago?"

I was beginning to suspect Virgil had more abilities than he let on because that was around the same time we were dealing with Bacchus. That or he had those bugs really well hidden and was constantly listening in on our conversations. One of these days I might remember to ask him.

Okay, you know I'm going to. Because I'm not okay with him spying on us, however he's accomplishing it, but there

81

are bigger fish to fry right now.

"Those don't do you any good in the pack," Ranger said, tapping the tissues.

"Why are you here?" I asked.

"I'm right under Virgil, and I can hear the two of them yelling at each other. You and the attack dog get in a fight or something? I might not have super hearing, but even I can tell when the argument is about one party leaving."

My heart stopped, the blood draining from my face. I started to get up, but Ranger's phone pinged. He halted me, one hand on my arm as he pulled it out, read whatever was there, and put it back in his jacket. "Yeah, no. Come on, get your shoes." His phone pinged again. Then it started ringing.

"Do you need to get that?" I asked, pulling my sneakers out from under the bed.

"No, it's just Virgil. And I don't feel like following his orders right now."

In the kitchen my phone pinged and then started ringing. Ranger walked off; I heard a drawer open and shut, then the ringing was muffled. Both phones were going at once. Ranger came back in and pulled me to my feet. "Let's go. We'll go for a walk until everyone calms down," he said, leading me to the front door. The knob wouldn't turn. Ranger yanked at it. "Motherfucker."

"I think Virgil might not want us to leave," I said.

Ranger turned and headed to the windows. "Fire escape."

"I don't think we have one."

The windows wouldn't unlock. Ranger gave up. "Guess it wouldn't matter anyway. Unless you want me to break the glass."

For a moment I was tempted. The whispers were tempted. If we left, it would be a small matter to leave Ranger in the dust and hunt down this god.

I've never done well with being told what to do.

A folded slip of paper slid under the door with my name

written on the front. I picked it up, opened it and read. Well, that was it then. I folded it back up, stuck it in my jeans pocket and sat down on the couch.

Ranger watched me. "What are you doing?"

"Sitting," I said.

"What's the letter?"

"Mine," I said. Because I wasn't sharing.

Ranger flopped down on the couch next to me. "Suit yourself. We just going to sit here?"

I waved a hand at the TV remote. "Help yourself."

Ranger sighed, leaned forward, and grabbed it off the coffee table. He turned on the TV and flipped through channels. "What do you watch anyway?"

"Movies."

"Very descriptive." He settled on some old Western. We watched it silently, the stilted dialogue and action putting it firmly in B-movie category. Ranger was fidgeting. Guess he doesn't do any better with being trapped than I do.

And I was still hungry. I got off the couch and went hunting through the fridge.

"Now what are you doing?" Ranger asked.

"I haven't eaten."

"I thought you were getting dinner with the future in laws."

"It didn't go well," I said, pulling out deli meat. Yes, we have meat in the fridge. I keep it separated from Greg's stuff. He says he doesn't care if it's in the fridge; he just won't eat it.

Which, yeah, if he tried to force me to adhere to his vegetarian diet, this relationship would've already been over. We came to the mutual agreement that when I'm unfamiliar with the food I don't mind him picking the dish for me, or if it's meatless.

What? I can be flexible.

"You going to make me one?" Ranger smirked.

"No."

He chuckled, got up from the couch, and grabbed an

extra plate out of the cabinets. "Guess I'll just help myself."

"You do that," I said, taking both my sandwich and a soda back over to the coffee table. He put away the sandwich-making supplies once he was done, picked a soda out of the fridge and came and sat back down next to me.

"How long you think we're stuck here?" he asked.

"Until they're done talking."

"That what your note say?"

"Essentially." It didn't say that anywhere on it, but the exact wording wasn't important. Okay, it was, but Ranger doesn't need to know that because he might see the information as his chance.

Oh, you're curious, are you? Sucks to be you.

We had been finished eating for a while; both of us were on our second soda, and the whispers had gotten bored and faded away before there was a knock at the door. Ranger surged up and over to it and yanked the door open. "Finally!" he said. "What's the fucking deal?"

Virgil was standing on the threshold. "Ranger, you can leave. I need to talk to Meg."

"I don't think so, you just locked—"

"Ranger," I said. "Leave."

He shot me a look, his mouth working. "Fine," he said, and he stomped out, slamming the door shut behind him as soon as Virgil was in the apartment and clear of it. He forgot his phone in the drawer.

Virgil sighed, standing back by the door, arms crossed. I stared at him from the couch. "Which message made you listen?"

"The note."

"Hmm."

"Where's Greg?"

"In my apartment. He's afraid to be around you." I flared up, my mouth opening to argue. "Don't," Virgil said. "He is scared he will attack you and that this time he won't be able to stop. He has never had to deal with these kinds of mental compulsions before."

"And you just happen to have tons of experience with this, huh?" I said, sarcastic and snappish.

"I do," Virgil said, heavily.

"Why, because you can do it?" I challenged him.

"I can," he admitted. "Not to the extent you can, and not to the extent that Bacchus apparently can. But I can influence, certainly. And before you ask, no, I do not use this on you or anyone else on the team."

I scowled at him because that was what I was going to focus on next. "What else can you do?" I asked suspiciously.

"Unimportant, and unrelated to now," Virgil said. "What I need is to find out if what the other gods can do has a range like yours. Until I have an answer to that, the best I can do is convince Greg to stay here, in my apartment, and he wants you somewhere he can't find you."

"No."

"Hmm. I told him you would get your back up about that."

"I'm staying."

"Indubitably," Virgil said. "I told him that too. He won't admit it at the moment, but he is relieved. I am requesting, on his behalf, that you lock the doors and keep the whispers around you at all times. Tomorrow, I would like the two of us to go speak to Ares about this situation."

"Okay."

Virgil nodded, strode over to the kitchen, and pulled the phones out, slipping Ranger's into his pocket and setting mine down on the counter. "I'll call you in the morning. Please lock the door behind me. Or I'll do it for you."

"Okay," I said, and he left.

I locked the door. Then I went to our bedroom and locked that one too. I called the whispers to me and set them in a perimeter around the room. The shadows and figures were darker than the real shadows on the walls. I sat down on the bed and pulled the note back out.

Virgil's handwriting, scrawled across the page, done in a hurry because his penmanship is usually neat and flowing: *Not irreparable, but only if you stay put.*

∞

There were waves, crashing against the shore, the sand hot against the soles of our feet where we stood out of the water's reach.

"Did we create the mortals, or did they create us?" he asked. We caught a glimpse of him, out of the corner of our eye. The gleam of sun on bronzed skin, long, loose curling, black hair.

He was standing too close for our comfort, his power crackling in the air.

"Does it matter?" we asked, a question for a question.

"No," he said. "In the end, they fear me, as they should." He stepped forward, toward the sea. "I need you for that."

∞

My phone startled me out of fractured dreams when it rang the next morning, and I scrambled out of bed to get out of it. I almost tripped over my own feet, caught myself against the wall, and then banged my shoulder on the doorframe of the bedroom as I ran for the kitchen.

You know, If I was a morning person, maybe my balance would be better that early in the day.

I snatched my phone off the kitchen counter where I had left it the night before. "Virgil."

"Not even a hello?" he said. "Before you ask, Greg is still asleep and under orders not to leave. I will be at your door in ten minutes. Don't be late."

He hung up

I dropped the phone and ran back to the bedroom,

wiggled my way into that stupid-ass catsuit, jeans, Greg's burnt sweatshirt, and fake chucks.

Hot mess hair bun, I do not have time for the curls today. Seconds later I was yanking open the front door just as Virgil had raised his hand to knock.

He smiled at me. "Eight minutes."

"Did you just test me?"

"Don't forget your phone," he told me, heading down the hallway. I ran back, grabbed it off the counter, shoved it in my jeans pocket, and went running after Virgil, who was serenely waiting for the elevator.

He took in my flushed face. "I thought we would grab coffee from one of the vendors in the park."

I nodded. "Great. Fine."

The elevator doors opened; we stepped in, and he hit the button for the garage.

"Ranger still mad?" I asked.

"No," Virgil said. "I gave him a – condensed, version of yesterday's events."

Two floors down the elevator doors slid back open: one of the other apartment building's tenants. I stepped away, putting my back against the wall. Virgil was silent, but I saw the way he adjusted his stance. The elevator stopped again, and the tenant got off on the first floor at street level. Neither one of us relaxed until the doors closed again.

We had reached the garage. "Cobra," Virgil said, striding out to the car. The doors opened for us. I climbed into the passenger seat and the door thunked closed behind me.

"Thank you," I said.

Virgil looked at me. "You're welcome. Seatbelt."

I got buckled because it would be stupid not to, but today Virgil surprised me. He pulled into traffic like a normal person would, actually yielding to right of way and waiting for the break in the cars he needed to make it without causing an accident. Or you know, just shoving the cars out of his way. He stopped at red lights and followed the speed limit.

He was making me suspicious. "Is there a reason you're driving like this?"

"Would you prefer the other way?"

"No."

He pulled up to the park, settling the car into a spot usually reserved for official vehicles.

"Your car is going to get towed."

"No, it's not," he said.

"Is this your influence thing?"

"Yes," he said. "Although I suppose I would simply do what Ranger does and take it back."

"I thought we were supposed to be the good guys?"

"I pay the fees. I just don't wait for them to be open to retrieve my belongings."

I snorted. We had climbed out of the car and were making our way into the park. We were back over by the lawns and botanical gardens. Once we stepped over the curb, past the decorative exterior fencing and headed down one of the paths, we spotted a coffee vendor.

I know, why are the food trucks only allowed at one end but the dude with the questionable food cart can go wandering wherever he wants?

Virgil got three coffees, handing one to me.

"You tired?" I asked him.

"No."

We were striding down the paths, working our way over to the lawns, and we came out at the end of them, where the lawn stopped before the pathways and city streets started. We stepped onto the lawn at the same time.

This time, Ares had the high ground. I wasn't sure if we should be surprised to see him, still here, skulking around the park. But I also wasn't sure what we would've done if he had been absent.

"That's convenient for us," Virgil muttered. I didn't think he had meant for me to hear that.

In concert, as if we had rehearsed it, both Virgil and I

raised a cup to him.

Ares acknowledged us with a tilt of his head, and then he waited.

"Guess we're going to him," I said.

"It would appear so," Virgil agreed.

We continued forward, reaching the hill and climbing. It was a good thing it wasn't a steep hill. When we reached the top, Ares stepped back to allow us room at the edge.

Virgil held out the extra cup of coffee. "A gift," he said.

Pleasure colored Ares's face for a moment before his stoic expression returned. He took the coffee. "As is my due," he said, his voice still harsh.

Virgil must've been doing some reading.

We stood there silently, the three of us drinking coffee, and eventually, Ares spoke first.

"You have questions."

"We do," Virgil said.

"Where are the other guardians?"

"Occupied," Virgil said.

Ares didn't miss much. "You mean at least one of them had an encounter with Bacchus."

"How do you know that?" I asked.

"He told me. He said you were rude. I asked him why he was surprised by that. You've always been rude."

"Did he, did that jackass—" I had to take a breath because I was pissed and sputtering. "Did he do that because I told him to go away?!"

"He did."

"That asshole is victim blaming me?!" I was going to rip him apart. I mean, I was already planning on ripping him apart, but now I was going to make it extra rippy. Because Greg was as much a victim of Bacchus as I was.

Ares didn't seem bothered by my anger. "He seemed to think he could help your attitude by making you less - frigid?"

"I'm not frigid!" Wait, why am I defending myself for that? I can be frigid all I want, and people should just respect that. "I'm not interested in whatever he had to offer, and he can just deal with it like a god damn adult instead of attacking people!"

Ares was watching me with those cool eyes. "You are offended."

"Yes, I'm fucking offended!"

"He'll set it right," Ares said.

"I very much doubt that," I snapped.

Ares didn't protest or try to defend him any further. He simply moved on. "I believe you had questions."

"What's the range?" Virgil asked, plunging ahead.

"Range?"

"How far out does the effect go when one of you compels someone? How close do you have to be? Does it wear off if you're not there? Can all the gods do it?"

Ares thought for a minute. "Mine is the strongest. It would stretch the entire length of the front line, and I was always present for it. Bacchus would wander room to room. But for his, generally the mortals were more than content to continue the activity even after his influence was gone."

"And Hera?" I asked, because I knew what she did to Hercules, what she had done to anyone associated with Zeus' "love" interests. A woman scorned doesn't even begin to touch on it.

"Present. And hers requires touch to set."

Don't let the jealous, extra proud goddess touch you, got it. Although, since they apparently don't need to be visible to set their compulsions in the first place, I'm going to be jumping at shadows now.

"Is there anyone else we need to be aware of?" Virgil asked, staying clinical.

"No," Ares said. "Well, the muses. But they're unlikely to bother you."

"I remember there being a lot more of you that could," I said.

Ares shrugged. "The mortals were inventive. I never

had sons."

I was thinking. He had to have left some things out, expecting us to work our way around to the question or just fail to get the information.

"What about monsters?" I asked him. "Can they do it?"

"Ah, you're asking about the sirens. They live below the waves. I doubt you'll encounter them. But yes, their singing certainly influences men."

"Men?" I asked.

"Just men," Ares said. "The tales did get that right. I assume it's because for so long women were not included in the seafaring voyages, so they specialized, and now their power is set, and they can't change it."

Well, good to know.

"I believe we're done here," Ares said, and he vanished, his empty coffee cup dropping to the ground.

I scooped it up. "Figures a god of war would litter."

"Hmm," Virgil said. He had his thinking face on.

"What?"

"Why did you ask about Hera?"

I could either tell Virgil the truth now or have him find it later when he did more reading. If he didn't already know. He had his fingers in a lot of pies, so I didn't know how much time he had for researching specific subjects, but it's not like Hera's envy was a secret.

I settled on truth. "To get back at Zeus, she went after his son, Hercules. She drove him mad, and he murdered his entire family."

He gave me a sharp look. "Don't say anything to piss her off." He started back toward the pathways, and I kept pace with him. His legs were longer than mine, so I had to speed up a bit.

"We don't even know if we'll run into her," I protested.

"I think it's obvious that at some point we will, and I assume you would like Greg to come back to your apartment. Do not be rude to her."

"You're not going to tell Greg that there's a goddess who could make him—"

Virgil cut me off. "If I tell him, he will leave. He won't risk you that way, and we need him right now. He needs to know it's safe for him to be around you, and it will be if you're not rude to the fucking goddess. And—" he continued before I could try protesting again, "if one of them is willing to use his power on the two of you to start with, I think we need to assume we're all at risk from them. *Don't be rude.*"

I don't think Virgil realized that Hera could get offended by shit I wasn't even responsible for, but I wasn't going to tell him that because then Greg definitely wouldn't come back.

I could keep Greg back from me if it came to that. It might ruin us, but it would be better than him living with the guilt of being the reason for my death for the rest of his life. I wouldn't inflict that on him.

Sometimes I look beyond myself and my interests.

We were at the car, and Virgil pulled the doors open. I settled into my seat, and he got in next to me but didn't start the car. He was quiet for a moment.

"I will talk to Greg when we get back. If you can, please wait in your apartment until I've assured him it's safe to be around you."

"Okay," I said.

"Thank you," he said, and he started the car. We spent the drive back in silence.

CHAPTER SEVEN

I was hovering in the living room, half seated on the arm of the couch, when there was a knock at the door.

I let the whispers go, tried to steadily walk to the door, unlocked and opened it.

Greg was in the hallway, head down, shoulders in. He somehow managed to look small.

"Virgil said it would be safe for me to come home," he said. Even his voice was small.

I flung myself at him, my arms around his neck, pressed as tightly as I could against his chest, his heart beating under my ear. For an agonizing instant, he stayed, stiff and still against me, and then he wrapped his arms around me and sank to the floor, dragging me with him. He clutched at me, shaking.

He was weeping, his chest shuddering. "Oh God, Meg, I'm sorry, I'm so sorry—"

I didn't think he would believe me if I told him he hadn't done anything wrong, so I just stayed with him, murmuring in his ear.

I'm not even sure of what I said.

Eventually he stilled, the weeping done, but still he clung to me. I think he was less traumatized when I died. I didn't know what to do. I couldn't ignore it; I couldn't pretend nothing had happened.

Do I have this kind of lasting impact on the people who survive what I can do? I had always thought of it as fleeting, something that only affected the moment and the minutes immediately following. Was I wrong?

Neither of us moved, and Virgil's door stayed closed. I wasn't sure if that was a good sign.

Finally, Greg lifted his head and looked at me. "Hi," I said.

"Hi," he said, and then paused, uncertain. "Can I come inside?"

"Yes," was all I said. What I wanted to say was, yes, you can fucking come inside, why wouldn't you be allowed inside? I didn't think he wanted to hear that either.

He lifted me with him as he stood and then gently set me on my feet. Then he waited, and I waited, and we stood there at the doorway, staring at each other until I realized he was waiting for me to go in first.

I'm only patient for so long. "You know I'm just going to stand here as long as you are, right?"

He watched me, looking flummoxed, which was better than guilty. "You always go in first."

"Correction: I go in first when I'm positive you're going to follow me."

"You want me to follow you?"

"Always," I said.

"Meg—" he started.

"I don't know what you need," I interrupted, because if I didn't speak up now, I wasn't sure I would have the courage again, "but I am not giving you up. I don't know how to reassure you; I don't know what to do for you. But if you try to leave me because of some asshole, I will hunt you to the ends of the earth."

There were tears in his eyes again. "Okay," he said, his voice thick.

"Okay?"

"Okay."

"Okay, glad that's settled," I said. I stepped backwards into the apartment. "Are you coming?"

He followed me, hesitating on the threshold before he stepped in and shut the door behind us. Then he hovered at the door. Normally I would've rolled my eyes at him, but I felt like I was dealing with a trapped and wild animal.

My phone pinged. I pulled it out, a text from Virgil: "Just do what you always do."

This time I did scoff and roll my eyes.

"What?" Greg asked.

"Virgil's being bossy again," I said, flopping down on the couch.

It must have been a safe subject because Greg followed me, easing himself down onto the couch, although he left me space he normally wouldn't have. I narrowed my eyes at him.

"Is there a problem?" I asked him.

"I thought—" he cleared his throat. "I thought you might need space from me."

"If I needed space from you, I wouldn't have opened the door," I said. "Do you need space from me?"

"I don't – I don't know," he admitted. "I'm afraid to be near you. What happens if he shows up and I get hit with that again?"

I wasn't sure if I wanted to tell him the whispers could stop it because then he would know I hadn't defended myself against him to start with. I was more worried about hurting him than what he could've done to me if he hadn't broken the compulsion.

"You stopped," I said. "You broke it."

"You screamed," he said. "I don't know if I could have if I hadn't heard you scream."

Oh.

He must have noticed the change in my heartbeat because he shifted, and his tone sharpened. "What? What aren't you telling me?"

"I could've broken it sooner if I had let them out," I

admittedly slowly.

"What?" Now he was angry, his eyes narrowed, jaw stiff. "Why didn't you? Why didn't you defend yourself?!"

"I couldn't hurt you." I was defending my decision as much as entreating him to understand. "I promised you I wouldn't use them on you like that, I couldn't—"

"Break it," he said flatly.

"But—"

"No, Meg. Don't you ever chance that again. You break that god damn promise and fuck the consequences. You don't *ever* not defend yourself against me like that again. I could've killed you!"

"Bacchus doesn't work like—" I argued.

"I don't care how he works! You've seen what I do when I'm not paying attention. I could have killed you no matter what his fucking goal was!"

I definitely hadn't thought that part through. I had assumed despite the compulsion Bacchus had trapped us in that I was as safe with Greg as I was at any other time. That if I had given in to it, I would have come out the other side as physically whole and undamaged as always. I'm not sure where either of us would've stood mentally, but otherwise, fine.

"Okay," I said.

"Okay?" he asked suspiciously. "Okay you'll break it, or okay you're just trying to distract me, and you have no intention of following up on that?"

"I promise to break my promise," I said, hoping he didn't realize I was hedging and that my intention was not to resort to the whispers immediately. I mean, yeah, if Hera showed up, fine. I'm pretty sure her compulsion would involve me dying anyway.

He looked like he didn't entirely believe me and he was trying to decide whether to call me on it. "I want you to have the whispers with you *any* time we encounter any of these gods. I don't care if Virgil thinks it's safe. And I'm not flying you anywhere until we're certain they're not just going to show up wherever we land."

I wanted to argue that. "I don't think Virgil's going to be—"

"I don't give a shit what he thinks about that. I would rather have you riding that fucking bike with Ranger than risk this."

I realized I was not going to win this argument, and the truth was Virgil would override any protests I had about it anyway.

"Fine," I said, crossing my arms and settling my feet on the coffee table. I glared at the TV.

"What are you doing?"

"Sitting."

"You're mad at me."

"No, I'm not."

"Then why are you wearing the death glare?"

I snorted. "I'm not mad at you."

"You're mad because I'm right."

I switched my glare to his face. "I am not." Because that also wasn't it. I was mad at Bacchus, and I didn't know how, but I was going to make him pay for what he did.

Greg sighed and scrubbed at his face. "Can we not?"

"I had stopped arguing," I pointed out.

He gaped at me. "You, you're infuriating."

"News to me," I said.

He shut his mouth and glared at me. I wasn't sure if this was an improvement, so I took my feet off the coffee table and scooted toward him. Since he was sitting by the arm of the couch, his choice was going to be stay put or stand up. He didn't move. I scooted again. He sighed again, wrapped an arm around me and pulled me into him.

"Are we good?" I asked him.

"We're good," he said. "You were really just going to let that keep going?" I could hear the disquiet in his voice, that I would ignore the cost to myself.

"No," I admitted, "Not forever. But you hadn't hurt

me, and then you stopped, so I didn't have to decide."

"You swear you would've stopped me?" I could hear the plea in his voice, the echo of *not this way*.

"Yes," I said. As long as my mind had been clear enough by the time I realized I had to, I would've. Although the whispers may have made the decision for me if it came to that.

He nodded. "Okay." So much relief packed into that one little word. He wrapped his other arm around me and kissed my head. "I think sex is off the table for a few days. I need–" he paused, started again, "I need to feel comfortable that neither of us is being forced."

"Okay," I told him. "However much time you need."

"We need," he said.

"We need," I agreed.

∞

We ended up spending the day on the couch watching old movies, spaghetti Westerns and samurai mostly. If we saw anything relating to Greek or Roman times, we changed the channel. Not even gladiator movies were allowed in our apartment right now.

I don't know that we were paying much attention to the movies we were watching anyway, at least not until we came around to *Monty Python and the Holy Grail*. We spent most of it laughing, although it got strangely silent and uncomfortable when Galahad ended up at Castle Anthrax. Fortunately, the tension relaxed a little once Lancelot rescued him.

They had *Robin Hood: Men in Tights* coming up next, and if I remembered correctly, things got a little dicey for Maid Marian, so I snagged the remote and switched the channel. I ending up on a home shopping network, which wasn't where I meant to stop it.

Greg was watching me. "You have something against Cary Elwes?"

"No," I said. "Just the Sheriff of Rottingham."

Greg was silent, but his arm tightened briefly against me. He checked his phone. "It's getting late. Did you want to order a pizza?"

"One of us would have to meet the delivery driver at the front door," I said. Greg scrubbed at his face. He was thinking again.

"And there's no way to be sure of who's on the other side of it. What if we go to Virgil's compound and hide out with his supplies?" he asked.

"You going to make Virgil drop us off?" I said.

He shoved his hair out of his face. "God damn it."

"We could make Ranger get the pizza," I offered. "If he's immune to the fear I put out, maybe he's immune to all the compulsions."

There was a pause. "You're a fucking genius," Greg said, and he kissed me before he was off the couch and bounding out the door.

I'm a genius because I found a loophole just so we could order pizza?

He came back, practically dragging Virgil with him, who looked like he had just been hauled out of bed. He was missing his duster, his shirt wrinkled, hair mussed, the imprint of fabric on his cheek.

It was the first time I had seen Virgil anything other than put together.

"Tell him what you told me," Greg said.

"This couldn't wait for a more reasonable hour?" Virgil asked.

"Some of us don't go to bed at 2:00 in the afternoon," Greg said. "Tell him."

"Okay, some of us don't go to bed at 2:00 in the afternoon," I said. If Virgil went to bed at that time, we were smack dab in the middle of his night. No wonder he sounded so irritated.

Greg shot me a look. "Seriously?"

Virgil was using one hand to rub both his eyes at the same time. "Meg, could you please tell me what has Gregor so excited he just had to wake me up?"

"All I said was we could send Ranger for pizza because he could be immune to all the compulsions since he's immune to mine."

Virgil stopped rubbing his eyes and lowered his hand. "What?"

"If Ranger is immune to me, he could be—"

"Immune to them all," Virgil's intake of breath was a hiss. "Why didn't I see that?" His hand was at his chin, brow furrowed. "Who can we test it with?"

"If Ares' range is as large as he says, I don't know that we would want to ask him," I said.

"Hmm," Virgil said. "A conundrum."

Because that left us with two choices, unless we could find the Muses or the Sirens. It was unlikely we could convince either of those groups to help, and Hera was no choice at all.

Greg wasn't going to like the choice we had left.

Well, I didn't either, but the asshole owed me. Yes, me, because he wouldn't care that he had offended Greg.

I saw when Virgil came to the same conclusion because his hand came down from his chin.

Virgil has never hidden much from Greg. If he was already hiding Hera's ability, he would be reluctant not to be open about this. Virgil's hand went back up, fingers rubbing at the bridge of his nose and his forehead. "This, no. We may have to let this one go."

Greg looked confused. "What? Why? If Ranger's immune, he's safe to be around Meg in the field."

"Bacchus is why," Virgil snapped. "We have three options. Ares has a range that is too large. The number of people who would die just so we can test this? That's not even a choice. Of the other two, I'm not sure we could even track Hera down, and she may already have it out for Meg. So that's not possible. That leaves us one, one option."

I could see the way Greg was struggling, his hands flexing. He looked like he was fighting the urge to start throwing things.

When we moved in, I had told him he couldn't break our furniture on purpose because of his temper.

"Do it," he said through gritted teeth.

Virgil was watching him, cool and appraising. "If you're sure. I'll need to bring Meg, and that's going place her at risk."

That wasn't the whole truth. Virgil may not have mentioned that Ares viewed it as a debt owed to me. Maybe Virgil hid more from Greg than I realized. It made me wonder what need-to-know details Virgil was hiding from me.

Greg swallowed, his jaw still set. "She says she can break his compulsion."

Virgil flicked his gaze over to me. "Can you?"

"Yes," I said.

"We're going now," Virgil said. "We'll meet with Ares and get him to bring Bacchus to us. I'll meet you at the elevator." He pulled out his phone as he walked away, already texting.

Greg pulled me to him, his nose in my hair. "Watch yourself," he said, his voice gruff.

I pushed back, leaning against his arms so I could look him in the face. "Always," I said. "You're purposely arranging things to make sure I can go fight giant snakes?"

"Would you let me put you in a tower?"

"No."

"Then I don't have much choice, do I? At least this way I can make sure you're teamed up with someone who can't be compelled into harming you."

"With Ranger?"

"Don't rub salt in it," he said, but he kissed me and then let me go. "Don't keep Virgil waiting."

I headed out the door and down the hallway. Virgil looked up from his phone. "We're stopping on Ranger's floor." He looked down the hallway, frowned and looked at me. "I'm going to have to stay out of range of whatever is going on. You will keep the whispers with you no matter what."

The elevator doors opened, and we stepped inside.

When the elevator stopped and Ranger got on, Maniac came with him. Virgil gave her a sharp glance and held a finger to his lips. She gaped at him, then narrowed her eyes. The elevator descended to the garage.

"Hummer," Virgil said. Both Maniac and I peeled away, headed for the passenger side. Ranger caught up to us on the side of the car, stepping so that he blocked us from the door.

"Uh no," he said. "Neither of you is sitting up front, I need to see where we're going."

"You get car sick?" Maniac asked him, one eyebrow raised.

"No—" Ranger started.

I ignored them both, stepping around to the other side of the car. I didn't have time for the argument.

I know, me not having time for an argument.

I could feel Ranger's eyes on my retreating back, and I had climbed in and gotten buckled before either he or Maniac had come to an agreement on who was sitting where.

Apparently my reaction had decided for him. Ranger climbed into the back in the seat next to mine. Maniac looked surprised by the sudden capitulation but shrugged and climbed into the front next to Virgil.

Ranger was leaning over as far as he could. "Are you okay?" he asked, quietly.

"I'm fine," I said. From the look on his face, he wanted to call me on the lie.

I spend a lot of time telling little white lies to the people I'm around. Maybe I should work on that.

I won't though.

Virgil pulled out of the garage to a chorus of honking horns, but the Hummer was already barreling through traffic, so I was too busy pressing back against my seat to yell at Virgil about it. Ranger stayed where he was, watching the cars and the traffic lights from the hump of metal in the middle of the vehicle.

"*We*," Virgil said cautiously, "should discuss the purpose of this outing before we reach our destination."

"What's going on?" Maniac asked.

"Does this anything to do with last night?" Ranger asked.

"What happened last night?" Maniac asked.

"The god Bacchus happened," Virgil said. "He has the ability to compel people into doing things against their will."

"What, like what Meg does?" Ranger asked.

"In a sense," Virgil hedged. "To put it delicately—"

"He's a sex god," I said bluntly. "And he tried to use his power on Greg and me."

Ranger was staring at me, wide-eyed, mouth open. "What?" he said weakly. "What happen – are you – did he hurt you?"

Virgil held up a hand, whether to forestall Ranger's questions or keep the car he had just cut off from hitting us, I wasn't sure. "Both Meg and Greg are physically unharmed—"

"Well, he would be fine," Ranger said heatedly. "You can't hurt him."

"But—" Virgil continued loudly, "it means Greg is a liability around Meg in the field. We need her partnered with someone who can't be affected, and unfortunately that means we have to go test that theory."

"No," Ranger said flatly.

"No?" Virgil asked.

"No," Ranger repeated. "You want me to let some jackass hit me with the compulsion to be a rapist? I'm not doing that; that's unacceptable."

"Meg's power can break it—"

"I don't care," Ranger said. "You shouldn't – you can't subject her to this. That's—"

"Unconscionable?"

"Whatever you want to call it. I'm not doing it."

"Ranger," I said, "please? People are going to be in danger. We can't just hide, and Greg needs me to be teamed up with someone who can't be forced to hurt me."

Ranger switched his glare to the metal hump. "Greg needs," he muttered. "What about what you need?"

"I need this," I said.

Ranger looked up at me, his mouth opening to protest, but whatever it was he saw in my expression made him hesitate. He looked back down. "Fine. But I want it on record that I'm doing this under protest and the second, I mean *the second* it looks like things have gone wrong, you hit me hard. Don't hold back."

"Thank you," I said.

"Don't thank me yet," he said, scowling out the window now.

When we reached Ford Harris, Virgil parked the Hummer on the curb. Not at, on.

"You're going to get towed," Maniac said.

"We'll just steal it back," Ranger told her.

She grinned. "Well, well, well. What would your golden boy say to that?"

"He's not my golden boy," Ranger said. "Besides, he's more of an attack dog."

The expression on her face changed, one of wary memory. "I think that description is more accurate than you realize."

We were following Virgil around the pathways back toward the lawns, and I was curious about what Maniac had said.

"What do you mean?" I asked her.

"Look, I know he's freelance and everything right now, but he used to have a leash." She shot a look at Virgil's back. "And they gave him targets. He might have just traded it for a new one."

"But villain targets—" I wasn't sure what the question I was trying to ask was.

Maniac was looking at Ranger and Virgil, edging closer to me, dropping her voice, and when Ranger noticed, he slowed to stay with us. She shot him a look. "Excuse you, but this is girl talk."

Ranger held his hands up, palms out, beseeching us, but he sped back up so that he was matching Virgil's position.

"Look, I don't know that he ever had 'collateral damage.' He doesn't seem like the type to blindly follow orders, especially with that whole, 'don't hurt civilians' thing he's got going on. But some of them, they don't care. You give them a target, and that's what they take out, no matter who's around. Some of you hero assholes aren't any better than the rest of us," she said.

I stopped, staring at her. "Then why did you switch sides?"

"Pay was better," she said flippantly.

"Meg, Maniac," Virgil said. We moved to catch up to him and Ranger. We were at the lawns, and there were still plenty of people around, but Ares was easy to spot; he was in the middle of the lawns, his back to us, and he was watching a group tossing a frisbee around. They looked like college kids.

Virgil made a noise. "There's too many people for this."

I wasn't going to be deterred. I pulled the whispers around me, tight against my skin. Both Virgil and Maniac took hurried steps back from me.

"Meg—" Virgil started.

"We won't test here," I said. "But Bacchus owes me, and Ares will deliver my message."

"One minute." Virgil said. "We have to—"

"The compound," I said. Because I knew what else Virgil had hidden down in there.

Bolt had made me curious when she made a comment about Virgil having secret passages. He had a way to contain people, down under the garage, and I wasn't above imprisoning a god.

I think that's when Virgil realized he wasn't talking to me alone.

"I won't try to stand in your way if this is what you want done, but I think you need to consider the ramifications—"

"We will go to war against any and all who touch what is mine," we told him.

"These are gods—" Virgil argued.

"So are we," but the whispers said it in sorrow. We turned, striding out across the lawn to reach Ares. The path cleared before us, people giving me confused looks even as they scrambled to get away from me. The compulsion of fear was more powerful than the need to confront the rude woman stepping among them.

Ranger was the only one who stayed with me. Virgil and Maniac had no choice but to hang back.

Ares turned when I was within a few feet of him. "Meg," he said. "An unexpected pleasure. But I take it this is not a social call?"

"No."

"Always business. It didn't used to be so."

"We used to be different," the whispers and I said.

"So you were," Ares said. "You used to be taller."

I snorted, giggling. "I don't think I've ever been tall."

He smiled at me, the corners of his eyes crinkling for a moment. "You have a message I take it?"

"Yes. Bacchus will meet me at a place and time of my choosing, and he will let Virgil test a theory. If he attempts to touch any of the others with me, I will end him."

"I don't think you could ever rid the world of debauchery," Ares said.

"No. But I will end his anchor, and then he will have to wait until he can find a new one."

"You are cruel. You know how bored he gets."

"That's not my problem. He shouldn't have touched what is mine."

Ares was looking over at Virgil and Maniac. "Is she one of yours too?"

"Yes," we hissed. We would not leave Maniac

unprotected amongst these gods.

"You're collecting quite the entourage. You used to work alone."

"We're never alone," we told him. I could hear Ranger shifting behind me.

Ares reached forward, and I almost jerked back, but all he did was twine fingers in my curls, studying them against his palm.

Which honestly, anyone else I would've yelled at them for touching my hair. Do I know you? Then don't touch my hair. Why do people do that? It's so fucking rude. I don't go up to you and start patting you on the head.

You know what, next time that's exactly what I'm going to do.

"This anchor suits you," he said. "I think had you not been what you are, you would have been at home in the woods with Artemis. You and she have much in common with the untamed."

"Well then tell her I said hi."

He smiled at me again, gently untangling his fingers and pulling his hand back. "I'll deliver both your messages. Although only one will bear you any fruit," and he vanished.

The one that bore fruit better be the one I wanted anyway.

There was a BOOM overhead.

Ranger had a hand on my shoulder as he tried to pull me down to duck; Virgil and Maniac had taken up a position back-to-back as they examined the sky.

I shook Ranger off, slapped his hand away.

Virgil looked over at me. "Meg, would you please—"

"You said whispers at all times," I said because they were agitated and clinging to me, and I didn't think I could get them to leave in this instant.

"No, that's fine. Would you please let Ranger help keep you safe instead of fighting him right now?"

I muttered and crouched down, and Ranger took a guard

over me. "This is ridiculous," I said. "Whoever did that is gone by now."

"No, they're not," Virgil snapped at me. He sounded stressed, which surprised me into silence.

Poor Virgil, I'm surprised he's not tearing his hair out daily dealing with gods and monsters, and now surprise flying visitors.

Maniac pointed. "There," she said. "Want me to blast him?"

We all looked. Someone was coming down over the trees, floating like he was standing in air, descending towards us.

Virgil swore. "No, but this isn't a complication we need right now. Meg, you can get up."

I stood, the whispers and figures swirling around me, curling through the air, smoke and ink, the shadows creeping out from my feet.

The man landed and walked the last few feet towards us. Everyone on the lawns was staring, the frisbee game forgotten. They were less interested in the god who had just been here.

Man, humans really are oblivious. Greg wasn't kidding when he said most people aren't that observant.

The man stopped, his jaw set, eyes hard as he took us in. I knew who he was even before he spoke. Even if he hadn't come in flying, I would have known. He and Greg had the same jawline, and it was easy to see where Greg had gotten his good looks from, although this man's were rougher, like he had been the reference model and Greg the refined and finished product.

"Where's my son?" he asked.

"Which one?" Virgil asked. "Because I'm sure Tony and Peter are at their homes. Maybe you should check there."

The man's eyes were roving over us, Ranger and I back far enough that I don't think he noticed I had slipped my hands behind my back.

"Which one is she?" the man asked, his eyes flicking between Maniac and me.

"Which one what?" Virgil asked, all innocence.

The man narrowed his eyes, stepping forward so that he towered over Virgil, but if he thought he was going to intimidate Vigilante, he was dead wrong. Virgil simply stared back at him, nonplussed. The man stood there for a minute, looming, slowly coming to the realization that he was not going to get the answers he was looking for from this group. I could see the moment he came to that conclusion because he stepped back from Virgil.

"I heard," he said, "that congratulations are in order." He pulled a business card out and held it out to Virgil. "If you would ask him to please call me. I believe Tony has provided me with an incorrect number." He waited, patiently, until Virgil reached forward and snagged the card. Then he took several steps back and took off.

Virgil tucked the card into a pocket. "Hummer. We need to discuss this new – development."

CHAPTER EIGHT

The discussion on the way back to our apartments had mostly consisted of Virgil swearing under his breath. When we had pulled into the garage, Maniac and Ranger climbed out, and Virgil twisted around in his seat to face me.

"We can't hide this from him," he said to me.

"Which part?" I asked. We hadn't met with Bacchus yet or done any theory testing, and I was planning on wiping the ground with him if he wasn't cooperative, so there was a lot to potentially tell. Or hide.

"Any of it," Virgil said. "We don't know if it's safe for anyone to be out in the field right now."

"Giant snakes," I reminded him. "It's *not* safe for anyone."

Virgil made a frustrated noise. "I know that. He knows that. But he's also used to being one of the biggest fish. I hate to bring it up, but Red Eye was the first time that I'm aware of where he was actually at risk. It rocked his world view."

I tamped down the shudder the mention brought up. *Fuck him, he's dead, I won.* I raised my chin. "I've already warned him what these monsters can do."

"Did he take you seriously?"

"Yes," I said. He had, hadn't he?

Virgil watched me for a moment. "Tell him again, and

keep telling him. Because he's as bad as you are about rushing headlong into the danger."

Weren't we all? It's what heroes do.

Ranger stuck his head back in the car. "Are you two coming?"

We both climbed out and followed Ranger and Maniac to the elevator. Virgil had his thinking face on again.

"Ranger, I'll call you when we have a development where we need you," he said. Ranger jerked his head, and then he and Maniac exited on Ranger's floor.

When the elevator doors opened on our floor and we got off, we both paused, because there was a gift basket on the floor in front my door. I could hear Virgil's sharp intake of breath behind me, but I was already stepping forward, crouching just within arm's reach of it to look.

"Meg," he said. "Don't touch—"

But it was too late, because I had reached forward, past the grapes, and the bottles of wine to pluck the card nestled within from it.

All it said was, "Call me."

No name, but I knew who it was. He was the god of the vine after all.

I surged up, slamming into the apartment door, knocking the basket over as I stumbled inside.

Greg wasn't in the living room where I had left him.

I ran for our bedroom, hitting the door with my shoulder as I scrabbled for the knob, and it popped open. I staggered forward; he was at the dresser, turning.

I collapsed, the relief turning my legs to jelly. He was by my side in an instant. "Jesus, Meg, breathe!"

Virgil had followed me; I heard his boots stop at the door.

They know where we live.

I had to focus. "You're here," I said. He was safe.

I think I had come to view him as unstoppable, unending, as invulnerable as his power physically made him, and that was a dangerous viewpoint to have.

I had warned him, but had I believed it either?

He had his arms around me. "Shhh, it's okay. I'm here, I didn't leave."

He must have realized something else was up because he was talking to Virgil over my head.

"What happened? Is Ranger not immune?"

"We haven't had a chance to test that," Virgil said. "We had to have Ares deliver a message. Meg, give me that card."

I hadn't realized I was still holding it, crumpled in my fist. The glossy card stock dug into my palm and left a slice in the skin. I handed it over to Virgil who took it, smoothed it out and read what was there before flipping it over to look at the back.

"Informative," he said.

"It doesn't need to be," I said. The whispers and I knew what it meant. Names have power, and all I would have to do is literally call to him.

"I seem to be missing something here," Greg pointed out.

"We appear to have to, call—" and Virgil switched what he was going to say because I was hastily waving my hand, "our unwanted friend here, and he will come to us. It looks like he left a peace offering?"

"Gift," I said. Which meant I couldn't just go chuck the whole damn basket in the trash.

"What?" Greg said, and he let go of me and left the room. "What the fuck!?"

"Don't touch it!" I yelled.

"I'm not going to touch it," Greg said, irritated and back at the door. "What are we supposed to do with it? I don't want it in the apartment. We can't leave it in the hall. Can Virgil float it out the window to the dumpster?"

"No!" I yelped, panicked. Both of them looked at me like I had grown another head.

Which, given the Hydras we had just encountered, might

always be a possibility.

"It's a *gift*," I said. At Greg's confused expression, the wrinkling of Virgil's brow, I made an irritated noise. "In the tales, refusal of a gift, any item freely given, by the gods always resulted in some serious consequences for the intended recipient." If I remembered correctly, but this didn't seem like something we should be risking after the last encounter.

"God damn it," Virgil said. "Do you have to accept it?"

"Unless we're going to trade offense for offense, yes," I said.

Yeah, I know, I just said I would go stick Bacchus in Virgil's dungeon - okay, containment space - but that was before I realized at least one of them knows where we live. Cooperation was going to end up being required.

And maybe moving.

"It's not coming in the apartment," Greg said. I was on the same page with him; I didn't want it in our apartment either.

"Do we have that option?" Virgil asked.

"I don't know," I said, honestly. "It could be that as long as it stays in this block of apartments it's considered accepted. And it's unlikely that any of it is inedible?"

"We should put it in Ranger's apartment," Greg said.

I snorted, giggling. "That's mean."

Virgil sighed. "I'm going to get a table and place it at the end of the hall. If we find out Ranger is immune, we'll store it in his apartment. If the compulsion can't affect him, I doubt anything that could've been done to the wine or grapes would affect him either." He left, and I heard his door open, the scraping of a table against the floor, and then muttering. There was the sound of a basket being set down, and then he was back. "Meg, would you get off the floor? We're not done with the news section of our show."

"There's more to today's three ring circus?" Greg asked. He had reached down and was pulling me off the floor.

I shoved at his hands. "I can get up on my own."

"But you weren't," he said.

Okay, so my legs were still a little shaky, and I was trying to hide that, but Greg had scooped me up anyway, setting me down on the edge of the bed and sitting with me, his arm wrapped around my waist.

"Are you two done?" Virgil asked. "Great. Your dad's in town."

"That's not a surprise," Greg said.

"Hmm," Virgil said. "I know, but he came by looking for you while we were meeting with Ares. He gave me his card for you. Said he thinks Tony gave him a wrong number." Virgil held the card out to Greg.

Greg took it, glanced at it, and tossed it at the dresser. It landed on the floor. "What else did he say?"

"He said he had heard congratulations were in order."

"Which one of my brothers told him?"

"Probably Tony if I remember anything about your family." Virgil looked at me. "Tony doesn't like me."

"You and me both," I said.

The corners of Virgil's eyes crinkled. "I knew there was a reason I liked you," he told me.

"Uh huh," Greg said. "We still have more important things to worry about. My dad can wait until this whole thing is done. He can wait until after the fucking wedding for all I care."

"Is that the terminology we're going for?" I asked. "Will that be our theme?"

"What? What do you mean theme?"

"Weddings have a theme."

"Like prom? I'm not having a prom theme for a wedding."

I could see Virgil's lips twitching, and he lifted his hand up, covering his mouth, but his shoulders were shaking. "Are you two done?" he asked, but he sounded incredibly cheerful about it.

"Right," Greg said. "Stop distracting us."

"Excuse me, but I didn't bring it up," I said.

"We're still off topic."

"Enough!" Virgil said. "The two of you, focus. Meg, when you've decided to take this seriously, let me know. I think we should reconsider going as far out as the compound. If they don't know about it already, we need to keep it an unknown. I think either a local warehouse or even the roof here would be a better idea."

"I don't want him that close to—" I protested.

"Meg, it's fine," Greg said. "I can go down a couple floors to stay out of range."

I looked him in the face, and he met my eyes, serious and implacable. "Fine," I said.

"Morning?" Virgil asked.

"Morning," I agreed. Virgil left, closing the front door behind him. I turned to Greg. "So, theme?"

"Courthouse?"

"You want our wedding to look like—"

"No," he said. "We could just go down to the courthouse and get married. Just us. We could ask Virgil to be the witness. No dramatics, no fuss, no themes."

It was tempting. But I knew he would regret not at least asking his family to be there. Although maybe he was worried that they wouldn't show up, and that would hurt more.

"Courthouse," I agreed. "But we have to at least give your mom and Peter the time and date. We'll make an appointment."

"Not Tony?" he asked, his lips twitching.

"Maybe Tony," I said. "But we should probably get rid of the snakes first. We don't need wedding crashers."

"Definitely don't." He gave my hands a gentle tug. "Come on, bed. Virgil'll probably come banging in at dawn."

∞

They were among the trees, hiding against the gnarled trunks of our olive grove, the drum-like rattle echoing around us.

"You can't tell her the why," she hissed at him. "If she knows the truth of it..."

He bowed his head, subservient to her wishes as always. They stood still and silent for only a moment and then they had spotted us, and together they vanished.

∞

Greg was up and making orange juice when I finally came wandering out of our bathroom.

Look, I washed my hair this morning. It takes time. We were planning on meeting with a god, and I had to do the whole make an effort thing. I needed him to take me seriously. I was even wearing jeans that don't have holes in them.

Greg noticed. "Who're you all dressed up for?" he asked. I settled on a stool at the counter bar and watched him without saying anything at first.

Bet you realized he doesn't need to use a juicer, manual or otherwise, to make orange juice.

He squeezed another half orange into the pitcher he was using. I put an elbow up on the counter, chin in hand. Some of the juice was dripping off his fingers. He paused what he was doing and looked at me. He leaned forward and kissed me, lips soft on mine. Then he pulled back and straightened up, twisting to face the wall and cabinets behind him.

"What?" I asked.

"The elevator," he said. "Back up, stay by the couch, and call them." He was already moving, positioning himself with his shoulder set against the door.

I did what he asked, making sure we had space between us, the whispers curling against my shoulders, figures and their fingers wrapped around my arms, the shadows pressing at my back. I could hear voices chattering as they came down the hall; whoever it was, they were loud and definitely not trying to hide the fact that they were here.

But Greg relaxed his stance, and waved a hand at me. "It's fine," he said. He sounded resigned. "Not a threat." I let the whispers go. Whoever it was knocked on our door, loud and brisk. Greg sighed and cracked open the door. "Hi, Brit, hi, Sandra."

What the hell were they doing here? And who gave them our address? For supposedly being a secret, a lot of people sure seemed to know where to find us.

"We're here to take Meg shopping," Brit said. I was still trying to figure out how they knew where we lived.

"Shopping?" Greg asked.

"Yes, shopping. Daughters-in-law bonding time," Sandra said.

Greg looked back at me. I was frantically waving my arms in an X, shaking my head. He grinned at me. "I think she'd love to."

I dropped my arms and scowled at him.

"Well?" he prompted. "What do you think? A day to relax?"

"We have an appointment," I hissed at him. "And snakes. Is now really the time for this?"

"One second," he told the two of them and stepped away from the door, coming up to me. I noticed he left it open. He set one hand on my arm, one on my face. His fingers were still sticky.

"You're going to get that in my hair," I told him.

"Is he really going to care if you make him wait another day?"

"No," I groused. He was probably off enjoying making mortals dance to his tune anyway. "What about the whole 'is it safe' thing?" Because Virgil might have an opinion on this.

"Take Maniac with you."

"Thought you didn't like her."

"She barbequed a giant snake for us. If you run into trouble, I think the two of you can take out any threat. Or at least delay it until the rest of us can get there."

"Why are you being all reasonable?" I asked suspiciously.

"You wanted a quiet life," he said. "Pockets of normalcy are the best I can do."

"You'll call me if something comes up? You're not going to leave Maniac and me at the mall thinking everything is fine while you're off killing Hydras?"

"Absolutely."

"Fine," I said.

"Don't murder them."

"What kind of person do you think I am?"

He chuckled and kissed me. "Watch yourself."

"Always," I paused, still looking him in the eyes. "I love you."

His eyes lit up.

Oh shit. This was the first time I had said the actual words out loud to him instead of vague assertions or coded phrases. The realization made my mouth go dry, my heart thumping, but all he did was smile at me.

"I know," he said, and he kissed me again, pulled back to look me in the eye. "I love you, too."

Someone rapped on the doorframe. "Yoohoo, you two are incredibly cute, but we're on the clock with the sitter," Brit said.

Greg chuckled again and let go of me, his hand on the small of my back as he gave me a gentle nudge toward them. "Go. I'll be here when you get back."

"I'm going, I'm going," I grumbled, but Brit and Sandra were making delighted squeals and gesturing me forward, so I rolled my eyes and sped up. They herded me out the door and down the hallway to the elevator.

"We have to make a stop one floor down," I told them.

"In case of hero stuff, we heard," Sandra said. "How exciting!"

Yeah, maybe to her. It wouldn't be that exciting if we actually ended up facing off against another snake. Well, not exciting in a good way.

"Why are we going shopping?" I asked them as the elevator doors slid open.

"Sandra and I have appointed ourselves your wedding planners."

"Wait, what?" I tried to back out of the elevator, but they were blocking the way, and the doors had already slid shut.

"Yup. We figured what with you and Greg having to run around handling whatever crazy shit is going down you two wouldn't have time to plan," Sandra said, "and before you ask, running away to Vegas isn't an option. Peter and I tried to do that. Oh. My. God. His mother's reaction when Tony tattled on us."

"I tried to warn you; you can't tell him anything. He's a gossip."

The elevator doors opened, and they herded me back off it. "Which door?" Sandra asked.

I marched down the hallway to Ranger's door and knocked. He pulled it open, looking surprised. "Meg? What's going on? Wasn't Virgil just supposed to text me?"

"Help me," I hissed, jerking my head back at Sandra and Brit. Ranger peered around the doorway at them.

"Yo," he said. "Who're you?"

"Brit and Sandra. The future in laws," Sandra said. "We're supposed to be picking up Maniac."

Ranger turned back to me and grinned. "Oh, yeah? Got big plans today, Meg?"

"Don't you dare—"

But he had turned away from the door and was bellowing over his shoulder. "Yo! Maniac! Meg's taking you out."

I heard muttering, rustling, and then Maniac was shoving her way past Ranger. "It better involve shots."

"Oh, we can totally do shots," Brit said. "The place we're going has everything. High end."

"I thought we were going shopping," I said.

"We are."

"Shopping for what?" I was extra suspicious now.

"Your dress, duh."

I turned back to Ranger's door because I was going to knock him out of my way, but he had already shut and locked it. I stared at it. Sandra hooked an arm through my elbow, towing me back toward the elevator.

"We don't even have a date!" I protested. Maniac was following in our wake. I half turned toward her. "Make them stop."

"Yeah, that's gonna be a no from me. They just promised me shots."

"What kind of friend are you?"

She looked surprised but pleased. "The kind who's going to force you into doing something good for you?"

We were back on the elevator, and Brit and Sandra had me firmly ensconced between the two of them.

"So, what were you and Greg planning on trying to get away with?" Brit asked me.

"The courthouse," I muttered. "We were going to tell you guys the date."

"Poor thing," Sandra clucked.

I started to flare up, my mouth opening.

"Oh, don't take that personally. We just want you to learn from our firsthand experience. Don't try for anything like that with their mom. Tony and I tried to get away with that one too. The fit over him being her first born and how she just wanted to see her boy married properly—" Brit shook her head. "I thought, oh my Lord, what kind of monster-in-law did I just hitch myself to?"

"So, we're going to make sure you do this properly from the start," Sandra said. "Because you do not have time for the dramatics."

I'm sorry, did they just quote me at me?

Look, I don't have time for other people's dramatics. Just my own.

Maniac was looking them over. "Are you two always

like this?"

"Oh totally," Brit said. "You get used to us."

That was a level of self-aware I was not expecting.

"Let's get down to business—" Sandra started.

"To defeat the Huns." I finished. It had popped out of my mouth unbidden and automatic. Both of them squealed again.

"Do you watch too many kids' movies, too?" Brit asked. "I swear, it's like I haven't seen a movie meant for adults in like, ten years."

I mean, yeah, I watch kid movies. But I don't have the excuse of having kids.

I cleared my throat and looked at the floor.

"We're going to have so much fun," Sandra said.

CHAPTER NINE

The bridal store was, in a word, POSH.

Have you ever been inside a well-known, high end bridal store? You know how they're huge? So many dresses, and usually there's a whole back-room warehouse-like area with all the extra ones? And the whole thing is crazy glamourous looking?

Yeah, no. I mean, this one was similar in terms of thick carpeting, soft seating, a whole serene color scheme. But that was where the similarity ended. This store was a lot smaller, and the selection was nowhere near that size.

But the gowns were definitely amazing. And not something I was willing to pay for. I had kind of planned on picking up a dress at Target if Greg was lucky.

The last fancy thing I wore was that little black dress, and I had thrown it in the trash. I couldn't associate it with anything else but that moment on the roof. So, I didn't even have anything that dressy anymore.

The consultant clucked over me, walking in a circle as she studied me. Give me gods and monsters any day because that scrutiny was just plain weirding me out.

"When's the wedding?" she asked.

"Undetermined," Brit said.

The consultant sighed. "Where is the wedding?"

"Also undetermined."

"Is anything determined?" the consultant asked.

"I mean, she's got the groom. That's the important part, right?" Sandra said.

The consultant didn't even smile. "Hmm. I'll go a pull a selection that I think will fit her frame," and she walked off.

"Where are the shots?" Maniac asked from the couch.

"One sec," Brit said, texting. "Sometimes I have to pull the brat card to get service here."

"How often do you come here?" Maniac asked.

"Oh, like, once a week. They're just lucky I didn't bring the kids," Brit said.

"You come to a bridal store once a week?" Maniac asked.

"Well, duh. My parents own it," Brit said.

Oh Jesus.

"Sweet," Maniac said. "They giving Meg a discount?"

"Oh totes. A hero wedding? They'll give it to her for free for the publicity."

"Wait, what?" I said. "My wedding is not a news fest!"

Brit waved me off. "Not that kind of publicity. For advertising." She was still texting. "I'm going to get the photographer who does the models. He'll be happy to squeeze you in."

"Does Greg know about this?" I demanded.

"No. But if he knows what's good for him, he'll just sit still for the ride," Brit said. "His mom is going to be thrilled. And won't that stick in Tony's craw?" She smirked.

"You're doing this to piss off your husband?" I mean, why was she even married to him?

"He's being a dick," she said. "That comment at dinner was totally unacceptable. He needs to get over the one upmanship thing he keeps pulling with Greg, and since he's not listening to me, and you totally deserve the in with their mom, Sandra and I are just going to railroad the two of you."

"Their mom doesn't like me," I said. I didn't think an in

with an actual wedding was going to fix that.

"That's a good thing," Sandra said. "It means she knows she can't run you off. She doesn't like Brit or me either."

You know, they were kind of starting to grow on me.

"Okay, the serious part," Brit said. "What kind of wedding were you thinking? Size-wise. And where?"

"Small," I said because I had expected it to literally be Greg, me and then maybe, like, 10 other people at most.

"How small?" Brit asked. "Are we talking minuscule, like no more than ten to fifteen people? Or, like, less than fifty people kind of small?"

"Minuscule," I said.

"We can work with that," Sandra said.

The consultant was back, gowns in her arms. She bustled by me to the fitting room off to the side. She poked her head back out. "I'm ready for you," she said.

I stared at her. "Ready for what?"

"To help you try on the dresses," she said, like it should be obvious.

"I'm pretty sure I can dress myself." I mean, I've been doing it for, what, twenty-three years or so? I know I could dress myself by the time I was four at least.

"Oh my God, Meg, go try on the dress so we can go do shots. Damn," Maniac said.

"I thought you were getting shots here," I said.

The consultant scoffed. "We don't do *shots*. Although I have a selection if you require drinks."

"We require drinks," Brit said. "And stop being a bitch, you're still gonna get a commission from this."

The consultant's face cleared, and she smiled. "Lovely," she said, yanking me into the dressing room.

"Hey!" I yanked my arm back. She ignored me, positioning me in the middle of the room.

"Strip," she said.

"I'm not into that," I said.

She rolled her eyes.

"Meg, don't make us come in there," Brit called.

Definitely would prefer the gods and monsters right now.

With a lot more poking, prodding and threats, the consultant got me into a gown and back out of the fitting room. She was at least smart enough not to comment on the catsuit under the clothes.

Look, I don't make things easy on people; in fact, I make them difficult for everyone around me. You know this about me.

Standing in front of the mirror, I had to admit I liked it, and that was kind of irritating. Light, gauzy, the fabric slid through my hands like water. The v-neckline and back were embroidered with leafy vines and inset with small pearls. You could see the shadowy outline of my body through the material. It was going to drive Greg nuts.

Which made it absolutely perfect.

"So, where are you thinking?" Sandra asked me.

"A rooftop," I said without thinking. "With olive trees." I wasn't sure where that had come from.

"It suits you," said a voice behind us, charming and smooth.

I whipped around, and Maniac came up off the couch, backing up toward me, hands up. Brit and Sandra half turned to look up at the newcomer.

Bacchus was standing at the door of the bridal shop, a different bottle of whiskey in his hands. This one was almost full.

"Brit, Sandra, get behind me," I said. They scurried over, hovering by the mirrors with the consultant. I turned my attention back to Bacchus. "What do you want?"

"You hadn't called me yet, and I was bored," he said.

"I was busy."

"I can see that. He must be special, for a mortal."

I didn't say anything.

He took a pull from the bottle, then pointed at Maniac

with it. "That one yours too?"

"Yes," I said, raising my chin.

"Shame," he said. "She's cute."

"Fuck off," she told him.

His eyes had a hard glint to them, although the corners of his mouth turned up. "Your collection tends toward the rude."

"They have that in common with me," I said.

He laughed. "So, I see." He stepped towards us, but Maniac and I stood our ground. He paused and took another pull from the bottle. "When you're not busy, let me know," and he vanished.

"Who the fuck was that?" Brit asked.

"Villain," I said. "If you see him anywhere you are, run."

"Got it."

The consultant cleared her throat. "So, uh, did you make a decision on that dress?"

∞

Brit and Sandra badgered me into ordering the dress. I let them, and honestly, I had to admit I wanted it.

They had dropped Maniac and me off at the front doors of our apartment building and told me they would be in touch with a venue and the available dates.

Maniac and I went inside, heading for the elevator.

"Are you going to tell him?" Maniac asked.

"Yes," I said. This wasn't a little white lie; it wasn't me trying to cover for a step with him I wasn't ready for. This was something I couldn't hide from him.

"Sure that's a good idea?"

"No." Greg had felt safe enough to send me out, and I didn't want to ruin that.

"Then why tell him?"

"Because then I'm lying to him. And he'll know it

anyway." That part was true.

The doors to Ranger's floor opened. Ranger got on with us.

"Have fun?" he asked me.

"No," I said. "Maniac never got to do shots. What are you doing?"

"You must've been disappointed," Ranger said to Maniac.

"I was."

"Excuse me, but what are you doing?" I said. The elevator doors to my floor had opened, and I was being herded again.

"Maniac texted me. We're your back up."

"I don't need back up!"

"You say that," Ranger said. They had managed to get me up the hallway, and Ranger knocked on the frame of the door rather than the door itself.

Greg pulled the door open and looked at the three of us. "What happened?"

"What makes you think something happened?" I said, but Ranger and Maniac herded me inside the apartment.

"Before you freak out, nobody died," Maniac said. Greg shot her a hard look. "What?" she said. "I figured that might be important to you."

Greg scrubbed at his face. "Meg, what happened?"

"We went shopping—" I hedged.

"Dude crashed the party," Maniac said.

"I was getting to that," I said.

"Yeah, via the long route. You have to rip this shit off like a band-aid."

"Do I want to have to ask which dude?" Greg said.

"At least it's not a new one?" I said.

"How many are there?" he demanded.

"How many hours do you have?" I asked. "Because telling you the names of all of them is going to take a while."

"Can I just get a quick count?"

"Around four hundred and twelve if you count the major and minor."

"Jesus Christ," Greg said.

"Good news is Ares already discounted two of them as never having existed so—"

"Great! Four hundred and ten!"

"You don't need to announce it. We can all do math," Maniac said.

Greg was scrubbing at his face again, shoving his hair back.

"Why don't you just get it cut?" Ranger asked. "Doesn't it get in the way, when you go rocketing around?"

"No," Greg said. "It doesn't. I'm getting Virgil; he's the only one who's not in on this party line."

"Did I hear my name?" Virgil said from the doorway. "Am I invited to give my opinion on this conversation?"

See, I knew Virgil wasn't going to be happy with Greg overriding the "call Bacchus in the morning" plan. What? I didn't say I wasn't complicit in the don't call Bacchus part.

"Meg needed—"

"Hmm," Virgil said. "From what I heard in the hallway this morning, Meg had very little say in what was going on. I know what those two are like." He turned his attention to me. "So what are they railroading you into?"

"They're planning the wedding," I muttered, looking down at the floor.

"She has a dress," Maniac announced.

"We're meandering again," Greg said, skipping right past Maniac's comment, but I saw the way his lips twitched. He was trying not to smile. "When did he crash the party?"

"At the bridal shop," I said. That definitely wiped any smile he had off his face.

"You're not going to throw that one away too, are you?" he asked.

"No, all he saw was the sample. The actual dress is safe." I didn't realize he knew where the little black dress had ended up. Hopefully he didn't ask about the heels.

"Is there more to this story? Why was he there?" Virgil asked.

"He said he was bored. And to call him when I wasn't busy."

"No, he said to let him know," Maniac corrected me.

"Same difference."

"Is it?" Virgil asked. "Or is there more meaning to those words?"

I sighed. "Back up a bit please." Ranger was the only one who didn't give me space. The whispers came, curling against my skin. I asked them: was there more to what Bacchus had told us in the shop? Or was it just a different turn of phrase?

They hadn't noticed anything in the encounter that would make them wary. He was legitimately bored and curious about what I wanted him for. I let them go.

"We're good," I said. "No double meanings."

Virgil nodded. "Okay, roof. Let's get this over with since we're all in the same place and currently don't have any calls. Greg, I want you in the air."

"What?" we both said at the same time.

"Show of strength," Virgil said. "He feels comfortable enough to show up in our home with gifts and to track Meg down while she's out. I want to make sure he realizes, compulsions or not, we're not going to let him fuck around with us."

"I don't—" Greg protested.

Virgil cut him off. "You will be out of range and able to see what's going on. And you will dive bomb him if it looks like things are going south."

Greg's mouth was working. "Fine," he said eventually.

"Good," Virgil said. He looked at us because none of us had moved. "What are you all waiting for? Go."

"None of us have the roof key," I said.

Greg sighed and took point, and we all followed him up

to the roof. Once he was out the door, he took off, up high enough that he looked half his size to me.

"You set?" Virgil called up. The pint-sized Greg waved down to us. "Good. Meg, Ranger, if you can go at least twelve feet out that way. Maniac and I will stay back by the door." I started to move but Virgil put a hand on my arm. "Can you keep the whispers with you constantly, or will that affect our ability to test this theory?"

I flicked up my eyes up, then back down to Virgil's face. "I'll keep them against my skin," I said. Virgil nodded, and I followed Ranger out onto the roof.

I did not call the whispers yet. "Five feet," I said to Ranger. He gave me a jerk of his head, and we both stepped away from each other.

The whispers came, sliding against my skin. Figures and their fingers, the shadows coalesced at my feet, a pool of black. "Everyone set?" I asked.

"We're a go," Virgil said from behind me, far enough away that he and Maniac didn't seem bothered by the fear in the air.

"Bacchus," I said, a call, a message on the wind.

Nothing happened. Ranger shifted; I could hear the scrape of concrete against his boots.

"So, is he coming?" Ranger said after a while.

"Give it time," I said.

"Should we call him again?" Virgil asked.

"No." He was only pushing the limits as far as he could before we could be angry with him. But we could be patient.

He chose to appear directly behind me, his voice in my ear. "You rang?"

I turned, chin raised. "You're in my bubble."

He smiled at me. "Am I now?" He took a step closer; my choice was going to be to let him touch me or back up. He brushed against me, his face hovering over mine.

"We can play this game all day," I said, "but if you continue to test me, you will lose." The figures had gathered themselves at my shoulders, their fingers curling down my arms, the shadows creeping closer to Bacchus' feet. He took a startled step back.

One point to me.

And he knew it. He took it well; I'll give him that. His laugh was genuine. He set his half-empty bottle of whiskey down on the parapet and took out his pack of cigarettes. "Anyone got a light?" he asked.

"I do," Maniac said. He looked at her; she was holding a flame in the palm of her hand.

"A Firestarter!" he said, sounding thrilled about it. He pulled a cigarette out and went over to her. He had it lit, an inhalation and exhalation of smoke before he said anything else as he came back over to me. "I haven't seen any of them in eons."

"Could you not?" I said to him. "I need space. I don't need cancer from your secondhand smoke."

"What do you care?" he asked. "It's just an anchor. You'll be gone before the rough shit anyway."

"No, I won't," I said.

He stared at me for a moment, the geniality gone again. "What did you do?"

I shrugged. "Ares didn't share that with you?"

"No, he didn't. He keeps his cards close to his chest. I thought some of the things you were saying were odd." He was eyeing me. "I should have realized on the roof something was off with your anchoring."

"Maybe you're just not that bright," I said, the words out of my mouth before I thought them through.

He snorted, laughing again. "Perhaps I would be brighter if I wasn't so blinded by your beauty."

I couldn't tell if he was flirting or teasing me. It could've been a reference to tales about the Furies, because they absolutely were not beautiful. Terrifying visage would be more accurate.

"You should drink less," I said. "Then maybe you

wouldn't be blind. It seems to be impairing your senses."

He was still laughing. "You are fun. How shall I repay my debt to you? I can plant groves of vines in your honor."

"Hardly anything that onerous," I said. I waved a hand at Ranger. "Compel him."

"As you wish," he said, a wave of his own hand. I could feel the craving in the air, and then it was gone. And nothing else happened. His eyes narrowed, and he looked at me. "What is this?"

"A test," I said.

"Hey, are we going to stand here all day?" Ranger asked.

"Can we do it again, Meg?" Virgil called.

"Try again," I said to Bacchus, but all he did was watch me. "What? You going to just give up?"

That goaded him. He hit Ranger with the compulsion again, and still nothing. And again, and again until he had marched up to Ranger and hit him directly in the chest with his power, but Ranger just stood there.

Bacchus turned on me. "What is this?" I could see he was on the edge of being angry. The whispers and I were smug, but we would need to use careful handling. We didn't really want a pissed off god wandering around the city.

"I can't touch him either," I said, coming up to both of them, strengthening the fear the whispers put out; it floated thick in the air. Bacchus backed up from me, but Ranger didn't move. I pulled the whispers back.

Bacchus was looking between the two of us. "Hmm," he said, because I had just given him information. "Close to the chest," he promised me. And then he vanished, leaving behind a full bottle of whiskey on the parapet.

He's going to have to stop leaving me gifts.

Greg landed next to me.

"He left us shots," Maniac said.

"You probably don't want to drink it, though," I said, reaching for the neck of the bottle.

"Wait," Ranger said. I paused, twisting to look back at

him, my hand still hovering over the whiskey. His eyes had taken on that blank look. "Snakes."

"Where?" Virgil's voice was sharp.

"The park, but I can't see where in the park."

"Lawns," Virgil and I said together.

"Greg, take Meg with you," Virgil said.

"What, no, I'm—"

"We need people evacuated and kept back," Virgil said, his voice calm, reasonable. "She can do that, and if Ares is near, he'll keep her protected."

"God damn it," Greg muttered, but he scooped me up and took off.

∞

We could see the Hydra from the air, and it must have just appeared because it was at the edge of the lawns where we met with Ares. It had reared up, swaying, people on the lawns screaming and racing away.

"Fuck," Greg said. "I'm going to drop you. Tuck and roll."

I hate this maneuver and the number of times Virgil made us practice it.

Greg dove; he was sweeping along the lawns, and then he let go. I dropped, chin to chest, and hit the ground with my shoulder. I ended up rolling a couple times before coming to a stop. I staggered up to my feet, pulling the whispers to me. Some of the people had frozen in place, staring at the snake and Greg as he slammed into it. The whispers and I set to work, flowing along the lawns between the people and the snake. The compulsion woke them up, and they ran, away from the snake and away from me.

I headed for the other half of the lawn to make sure that was clear.

There was only one person standing there, small, dressed in a bright orange shirt and neon green shorts. A child who couldn't be more than four, and he was staring up at a second snake that had appeared, rapidly gaining size.

The whispers, figures, shadows and I surged forward. The snake was growing ever higher, and it was hissing, its mouth opening and fangs extending.

I was between the two, and the figures and their fingers had unfurled, slashing at the snake's coils, digging at the flesh within. It shrieked, twitching its body back, and I turned to snatch up the boy. He was crying; the fear in the air had scared him, but I couldn't help that. I had to get him off the lawns.

The Hydra howled. I was clutching the kid to my chest, but I wasn't going to be fast enough to get out of the way.

My feet left the ground, someone swearing against my ear, and then we crashed into the bushes and trees past the lawns. Whoever had grabbed us was staggering away, the branches crunching, cracking and snapping as they scrambled to get away from me and the screaming child. He was still swearing.

It wasn't Greg's voice.

I let the whispers go and looked down at the brown eyes looking up at me. Full of tears, his face was crinkled, snot nosed. "Hey kid," I said. "Did I scare you?"

He nodded, sniffling and cried some more.

I had no idea what to do, but whoever had just kept us from getting eaten crunched back over to us. "You should keep talking to him. Use a soothing voice."

"I don't do soothing," I said.

Greg's dad was looming over me. "No, you don't seem to. Who are you?"

"Vengeance," I said. I had one hand on the kid's back, rubbing up and down. He said be soothing. I'm trying at least.

He was watching my hand.

"What?" I snarked. "Never seen a lady with some stranger's kid before?"

"That was my mother's ring."

"Wonder how that got there," I said sarcastically. "I

would like to find this little guy's parent or parents and get back to the giant snakes fight."

"I'll take him," he said.

I hesitated.

"I can cover more ground," he said impatiently.

I patted the kid on the back. "Hey, kid, can I send you with the guy who can fly? Do you know your parents' names? Address?"

Greg's dad made an impatient noise. Dude needed to chill. "I think I can figure out who his mom is."

"Yeah?" I asked. "What if he's here with his dad? Came with a school group?" Not to mention all the other possible family unit combinations. But we had two giant snakes to contend with, and I don't have time to waste listing them out for this guy.

Greg's dad looked flummoxed. It was strange seeing an expression so similar to Greg's on someone else's face. His expression cleared. "I can figure it out. Give him to me."

"You have a name?" I asked coolly. Giant snakes, yes, but I'm not handing a kid over to someone who just runs off on their own family unless I know how to track him down.

I will literally send Ares after him if he doesn't get this kid delivered to his family.

"Flightpath," he said. He held out his arms.

"You wanna fly? Like an airplane?" I asked the kid. He nodded, going from terrorized to excited in the space of a breath.

Damn, wish I could switch moods that fast. I just go from irritated to pissed off, and then I stay that way for hours. I should work on that. I handed him over, and Flightpath took him, settling him snug against his chest, and then he took off.

"Ass," I muttered. "Not even an assist up."

I got myself up out of the bushes and onto the path. Greg's sweatshirt had a few more holes in it. I was headed for the lawns and whatever was happening there with both snakes - at the very least I needed to make sure they stayed on the grass -

when something moved.

I froze. The whispers were against my skin because out of the corner of my eye I could see the bright green of a different kind of snake, and there were multiple voices hissing at once. I shut my eyes. This was not good. This was so not good.

The whispers, figures and shadows were swirling around me, and I didn't know which direction was going to be safe to take. I hesitated too long because the thing shrieked, and I heard it start to move.

I darted forward, eyes open. I needed to see where I was going.

But that thing was fast.

It snatched my ankle, and I hit the ground hard, slamming into it on my shoulder because the thing had yanked my foot out from under me and was pulling me back toward it and up into the air, swinging upside down as it reared up. My hands were over my face; I couldn't look it in the eyes, or I was doomed. The whispers howled, screaming and I heard the figures fingers as they clawed at it: nails on a chalkboard, a screeching noise, combined with the sound of steel striking flint.

Oh fuck.

But the fear hit him too and he dropped me.

Seriously, Greg was right, bank robberies and regular jewelry thieves any day.

I hit the ground again, shoulder and back, and I rolled onto my stomach, eyes on the ground. I had to figure out where he was and run in the opposite direction.

The whispers were still hammering the fear into him, and I could hear his own claws scrabbling against his scales.

Why is the Gorgon who turns people into stone made of motherfucking stone? How is that fair?

But the noise he was making let me know where he was, so I twisted to my left, scrambling to my feet, and I ran. I didn't have a way to hurt it; the fear couldn't make it hurt itself, the figures couldn't get through its skin, and I couldn't just stand here waiting for it to run away. Where could I lead it to keep it contained?

I needed a mirrored surface. Then I could at least see where it was in comparison to me. If it saw its own reflection, would it turn itself into a statue? Or would that not work on it because its skin was already stone?

I could hear it slithering after me, the scraping noise it made as it came down the pavement of the path. I had gotten far enough away from it that the fear was no longer bothering it.

I had run too far; I had come out at the streets, and I had to stop because there were people here. Shit, where could I go?

I could hear the roar of the Hummer's engine, and I know the way Virgil drives, and where he was going to be stopping. I let the whispers go.

I'm sorry Virgil, don't be mad at me, and don't tell Greg I did this.

The thing behind me snarled. I darted forward, into Virgil's path, and it followed me.

Virgil bumped me out of the way and with a crunching, shrieking bang the Hummer hit the thing head on. I staggered, narrowly avoiding getting hit by another car, but it had slowed, so I think Ranger had something to do with that. I managed to regain my footing and turned back. The entire front end of the Hummer had been smashed in. The metal was crumpled, bowed, split.

The Gorgon was gone, a manhole cover left in the street. The thing went into the sewers. Damn it, I made Virgil wreck his car for nothing.

Virgil had to kick his door open; that was how far up the damage had managed to spread. He was climbing out. "What the fuck, Meg!"

"Sorry," I said.

"My car!"

"Thought you didn't wreck," I told him.

"You," he sputtered, and he was pointing a finger at me. "That was dangerous! That was stupid!"

"There's two Hydras on the lawn," I told him, because I had to head him off before he really got going on me.

"Fuck," he said. "We're not done here. Ranger, grab the swords. And, Meg, after these things are dead, I'm telling Greg what you did."

At this point the four of us were running up the path back toward the lawns. "I should make you wait at the fucking car," Virgil was half snarling.

"I'm sorry about the car," I protested.

"I'm not mad about the car!" he said. We had reached the lawns, and Maniac raced ahead of us, flames streaming. The snakes were hissing and screaming as their flesh blackened and burned.

Greg was still in the air, keeping them occupied, and he wasn't alone. Flightpath was up there with him.

He better have left that kid with the right people.

Greg slammed into the head of one of the snakes, dragging it to the ground. Flightpath was keeping the other one up and distracted. Ranger and Virgil were moving forward to deliver the swords and keep the snake pinned.

At this point I was superfluous, and I was cool with that. I'm not used to having to put in this much effort with hero work.

I got to sit back and watch the show while they chopped off the first snake's head and Maniac burned the flesh after.

Fortunately, the other Hydra didn't seem to be thinking about the fact that it should help its brethren because it was going to be next otherwise. It was too busy trying to catch Flightpath, who was flying switchbacks through the air. It kept weaving and swaying, its attention fully centered on him until Virgil grabbed it with his power and pulled. Then it fought back. Greg had to get into the air again and drag that head down too.

Once they were done, the air stank. Greasy, dark smoke

was roiling from what was left of the snakes.

I wandered over to them. "That was fun."

Greg looked at me. "Why are there leaves in your hair?"

"Couple reasons really."

Flightpath had landed next to us. "Gregor."

"Fortress," Greg corrected him.

"Fortress," Flightpath said stiffly. "Son," he added. "I heard you're going to be getting married."

Greg scowled at him. "Who told you that?"

"Your brother," Flightpath said.

"Which one? So I know not to invite him."

"That seems like an extreme attitude to take since I just kept your fiancée from getting eaten."

Greg wrapped an arm around my waist, his fingers flexing against my hip. "Did you almost get eaten?"

"There was a kid and a second snake," I said.

Virgil sighed. He may have just decided not to tell Greg about the car maneuver.

"Would you like to introduce me to your team?" Flightpath asked.

"No," Greg said.

"They're my team," Virgil said.

"Who are you?"

"Vigilante."

"Thought you worked alone."

"Not anymore."

We were long past the awkward stage, and Flightpath seemed to realize that. He backed up a bit. "I would appreciate if you would call me when you're ready. To discuss things, over coffee. Or I could take you and Vengeance for dinner so we can get to know each other." Then he took off.

"Don't hold your breath," Greg muttered.

"We all need to go over to the Hummer and figure out what we're doing from there," Virgil said, "because it needs a tow."

"What happened to the Hummer?" Greg asked.

"Gorgon wrecked it for Virgil," I said. What? Technically it's the truth.

We were all walking, the five of us headed for the street. When we reached the Hummer, Greg shoved his hair back. "How exactly did the Gorgon wreck it?"

"It just jumped out in front of it. Craziest thing," I said.

Maniac and Ranger both snorted. Virgil sighed.

Greg turned to Virgil. "Thought you didn't wreck?"

"Is it wrecking if you hit it on purpose?" Virgil said. "Ranger, can you fix this?"

"No, outside the limit," Ranger said, studying it, his eyes having gone blank.

Greg scrubbed his face. "Where do you need me to take it? I can get the metal straightened back out, but honestly the whole thing is fucked."

"There's a scrapyard out off highway nine; take it there. And see if he has one to replace it with. Just don't let him try to upsell you on a tank."

"Why would I even consider a tank?" Greg said, but he lifted the Hummer up and took off with it.

Virgil looked at the rest of us. "Taxi?"

"Taxi," Ranger said.

CHAPTER TEN

We were back at the apartments before Virgil said anything else. All four of us had made it up to the hallway of the top floor before he turned toward me. "You, your apartment."

Ranger opened his mouth and Virgil held up a hand.

"No, I do not want your opinions on this right now."

"I don't know what you were expecting her to do with that thing chasing her," Maniac said. "I would've made you wreck too."

We all stared at her. She shrugged. "What? You all were already teasing him. I can't join in?"

"If I hit you with the car, would you have been able to get up and walk away?" Virgil asked.

Maniac thought about it for a minute. "Hmm, probably? I mean, might need a minute. That Hummer was tough."

"Well, Meg wouldn't. So, if you would both kindly butt the fuck out." He motioned at my door. "Meg, if you would, please, so we can discuss your reasoning behind the stunt you pulled."

I hesitated because I was surprised by and appreciated the back up from Maniac and Ranger, but Virgil seemed to have calmed down, so I didn't think my dressing down was going to involve any more threats to tell Greg.

And the reason why I had run into traffic was something everyone was going to need to hear.

"His skin was too tough for me to get through," I said.

Virgil sighed. "Here?"

"They need to know," I pointed out.

"Then technically we should be waiting for Greg to get home," Virgil said.

"His skin was too tough?" Ranger asked.

"Like it was made of stone," I said. "The figures couldn't hurt him."

Virgil was rubbing his eyes with one hand again. "Great. Did he react to the fear at all?"

"Definitely," I said. I mean, he had at least dropped me.

"Is he - what was the other thing you had asked Ares about? A basilisk?" Ranger asked.

"No. He's a Gorgon. He's the thing sending out the Hydras," I said making an irritated noise because they wouldn't have the information I did. "Backtrack. Medusa is a he, and he's a Gorgon. They're a type of monster; there were three according to history, and Medusa was one of them. Apparently, he can create Hydras, which was *not* in any of the tales I know."

"Medusa is made of stone?" Virgil asked.

I shrugged. "That's what it sounded like. I didn't touch him directly. I was too busy for testing."

"From the top," Virgil said.

"Which top? The top where Greg dropped me off or the top where I found the Gorgon?" Well, technically the Gorgon found me.

"Guess," Virgil said.

"You should just put one of those little cameras on me and then you wouldn't need to make me run through all this."

"Oh, but I would."

I muttered to myself for a minute, and Virgil leaned back against the wall, arms crossed. Maniac was swinging her arms at her side. Ranger was imitating Virgil across the hallway, leaning against the wall, arms crossed; the only difference was that he had one leg drawn up, boot resting against the wall itself.

"You're going to scuff the paint," Virgil told him. Ranger shrugged. "If you insist on scuffing the paint once our headquarters are finished, you will get to do the repainting," Virgil said sternly. Ranger took his foot down.

There were footsteps coming down the stairs. Virgil and Ranger came off the walls, and Maniac turned to face the stairwell door.

Normally we would have assumed it was Greg, but since we had at least one god who felt it was okay to just show up in our hallway, no one was taking chances.

Greg came through the door, and the four of us relaxed. Ranger leaned back against the wall but made sure to keep his boots on the floor.

"I had to place an order for a new Humvee," Greg told Virgil. "The only thing he had was a Jeep, and he couldn't remember if it came with the doors."

Virgil sighed. "Remind me to check that the army isn't missing one once he calls to tell me the order is in."

Greg chuckled. "I got the impression that it just might be missing one already. He just didn't have it on hand yet."

"For good guys, you steal an awful lot of shit," Maniac said.

"Technically, we didn't steal it. We just purchased goods of dubious origins," Ranger told her. "We're as much a victim here as the US army is."

"I don't think the army is going to view it that way," Maniac told him.

"Could we please?" Virgil said. "The origins of the Hummer are not on the table right now. Meg, the Gorgon?"

"What about a Gorgon?" Greg asked.

"The part where Meg found one," Ranger said.

"Beep, beep, now who's a bus?" I said.

"I did not just throw you under one, but if you're going to be that way—"

"Enough!" Virgil said. "It's like herding cats with all of

you. I regret the day my team ever became a reality. Meg, from the top please."

"You know you love us," Maniac said. At the look Virgil shot her, she cleared her throat. "Sorry. Last word, I swear."

I wasn't sure when Maniac had become an official team member because I hadn't been there for that invitation. I hope Virgil has a space in headquarters set aside for her. He hadn't mentioned what the extra floors were for, although expansion would make sense.

I was getting off track. I was supposed to be telling Virgil how I found Medusa - Medusus? Guess we should stick with Gorgon or Medusa for now rather than name quibbling.

"Meg," Virgil said.

"Well, Greg dropped me off. There was this kid and a second Hydra, and Flightpath got us out of the way. He took the kid, and that's when the Gorgon showed up. You can't look this thing in the eye, so I ran because I needed somewhere he could get stuck or a mirrored surface, but I went the wrong direction. And then you wrecked into him."

Virgil had his face in one hand. "Meg, at what point did you realize he was stone?"

I flicked my eyes over at Greg, then back to Virgil. "Um, when he grabbed my ankle. I was trying not to look at him, and the figures went after him. I could hear their fingers scraping against his skin. He dropped me, though."

"And that's when you ran from him?"

"I mean, I tried to run from him from the start."

Greg was scrubbing at his face. "You went the wrong direction?"

"I wasn't trying to go for the street. There were people in that direction."

"But, *conveniently*, Virgil wrecked into him at that point," Greg pointed out. "I know that thing didn't jump out there for no reason."

"It gets blurry," I hedged.

"Meg—" Greg started.

"You keep telling Meg what she shouldn't have done," Ranger snapped. "But she's fine. I don't know that you should get to judge what her choices in the moment should've been. She had a solution, and she used it."

The two of them were squaring off against each other, Ranger having come off the wall again.

Greg was snarling at him. "You don't get to make judgements about this. I've almost lost her twice now, and I'm not chancing losing her again."

"Maybe you deserve to lose her if you're going to keep shoving her in two different directions. You can't expect her to do this hero shit and always stay safe at the same fucking time!" Ranger shouted at him.

But Greg wasn't shoving me anywhere. I was choosing to show up for this shit. If Greg had any say in it, I would be at home staying safe, so I stepped between them.

"We're done here," I said. "No one pushes me anywhere, and if you two don't knock it off, I'll make you."

The tension was still in the air. "Excuse me, but I'm the god here," I said.

Greg's lips twitched. "You're the what now?"

"That doesn't make you the boss of me," Ranger said.

"I'm the boss of whomever I damn well please," I said.

"You going to try and boss Virgil around too?" Ranger asked.

"I'm right here," Virgil said. "Can we please focus?" The tension was still there, coiled and waiting, but the impending altercation between them seemed to have retreated for the moment.

"What I was going to say," Greg said, shooting a glare in Ranger's direction, "was that you led him into the street on purpose, didn't you?"

"It seemed like a reasonable solution at the time."

"Because it was," Ranger said.

"I didn't say it wasn't!" Greg growled.

"Stop it," Virgil said. "Meg's right, this is over. If the

two of you can't have a discussion of events without snipping and sniping, go somewhere else."

"You all need to work on your communication," Maniac said. She didn't quail under the matching glares Greg and Ranger shot her. She just glared back at them.

"Meg, please continue. Why did you take it into the street?"

"Because you were there with the Hummer. I wouldn't have done it otherwise. I didn't expect him to get up from that."

"I'm not sure he went down in the first place," Virgil said. "How did he die in the original tale?"

"Perseus cut off his head while he was sleeping." I was pretty sure Virgil knew exactly how he died and only wanted me to say it for the rest of the class.

"Where did he go after Virgil hit him?" Greg asked.

"The sewers," Virgil and I said together.

"I suspect that's where he's nesting if that was his first choice of places to go when fleeing," Virgil said.

"I hate the sewers," Greg muttered.

"Not enough space for you down there?" Ranger asked snidely.

"No," Greg said. "There's not. I could take out too much of the infrastructure without meaning to."

"Huh," Ranger said. I don't think he was expecting a serious answer from Greg with the tone of voice he had used.

"At least he's not wandering around above ground turning people to stone," Virgil said.

"Nope, just setting Hydras free in the park," I said.

"Okay. We have two choices: track him down in the sewers or wait for him to show back up."

"We're going to need mirrors," I said. "Because we don't want to be blindly going around corners."

"If we track him down in the sewers, we need to end him quickly, before I fuck up something I shouldn't have hit," Greg said. "There's not enough space down there for me to be wrestling snakes into submission."

"We want him taken out quickly anyway," I said. "And to do it while he's sleeping. I don't know about you, but I don't think spending eternity as a statue would be comfortable."

"So," Maniac said, "we're going to track down a snake monster that can turn you to stone, that we can't look directly at, and we need it to stay asleep to kill it?"

"Basically," I said.

"Excellent," she said. "I'm packing snacks for the trip."

∞

At that point the party broke up. Virgil went to research the best way for us to go wandering around the sewers with mirrors and how we were supposed to see down there without waking the Gorgon up with a bunch of lights. He also got updated blueprints for the sewers and subways. He didn't trust the thing not to have broken through a tunnel wall somewhere. The discussion was trending toward locating wherever the Gorgon was nesting and then setting up observation to see when he came back rather than hoping we just happened to stumble upon him while he was asleep.

Greg closed our front door behind us before he said anything else. "So, Flightpath rescued you?"

"Assisted," I said.

"Hmm." He pulled me into his arms, planting his nose in my hair. "Don't you dare lead that thing into Virgil's Cobra. I don't think he'll survive the heartbreak if that car gets wrecked."

"That car is a classic, and I would never risk it that way," I said.

He chuckled and then was silent for a long moment, his arms tightening around me. "Did you want to go get dinner with my dad?" he asked.

"Do *you* want to get dinner with your dad?"

He sighed, loosening one arm to shove his hair back. "I

don't know."

"You know you don't owe him anything for getting me out of the way."

"That's not—" he sighed again. "I don't know that he sees it that way."

"Because you don't know him. And whose fault is that?" I pointed out. "Because it's not yours."

"But he's asking for a chance to know me now."

"Hmm," I said. I was trying not to let my own opinion of him color what I said to Greg. I mean, I probably wasn't succeeding, but it was Greg's choice, and I didn't want to him to make his decision based on what mine would be. What I wanted to know was why Flightpath didn't ask for that chance sooner.

"He did come searching me out," Greg said. I could see he was wavering, looking for a reason to justify meeting up with Flightpath. I could understand why. Greg has always been more forgiving than I am.

Well, it's hard for me to be forgiving when I am what I am. But I can't force other people to hold the same grudges.

"More than once," I said. "If you want to go get dinner with him, I'll be right there with you." Ripping him apart if I didn't like his answers.

"Thank you," he said. "I'll call him in the morning to set something up."

"Are you going to go for as awkward as possible or casual?" I asked.

He chuckled. "I hadn't decided yet." He was sliding his hands under the sweatshirt. "You're going to need a new one of these if you keep putting holes in this one."

"I should probably just get a tougher jacket or something."

He didn't answer me because he was busy pulling the sweatshirt over my head, and then he was pulling at the zipper on that damn catsuit. His lips were on my neck, and he was peeling the suit off my shoulders. Then he stopped, pulling his head back. "When did that happen?"

I had to crane my head down to see what he was looking at. "Huh," I said, staring at the black and purple bruise spread across my left shoulder. "I don't know. I hit a lot of things this afternoon." The Gorgon had dropped me pretty hard.

But Greg was looking at the outfit. "Did this thing get compromised? We can't send you out in compromised equipment."

"I don't think it's a miracle worker," I said. "I think it's mostly there for the bullets."

He was grinding his teeth. "Fucking gods and monsters. I liked it better when you were a megalodon and not a fish."

"I was never a megalodon," I said. "Just another one of the sharks."

"Megalodon is a shark."

"He's a monster."

"Are you arguing semantics with me again?"

"Absolutely."

He sighed, turned me around and nudged me toward the couch. "Sit, I'm going to get a compress and the Arnica for that thing."

"It doesn't even hurt," I protested.

"I will make you eat pineapple. Sit."

"I think that's an old wives tale, and I hate pineapple."

"Sit."

"Fine, I'm going, I'm going," I muttered, sitting on the couch after I took the time to peel off my jeans and the rest of the outfit.

What? He started it. If he's feeling safe enough, then I'm game.

He came back from the bathroom with his supplies for my bruise and sighed, but I could see he was fighting not to smile. "Really?"

"I was checking for other bruises so we don't have to repeat this later," I said.

"No, you weren't," he said, "because you didn't notice

the one on your ankle, did you?"

I looked. "Huh. I did not." That was a lie. I did notice it, and it was why my feet weren't up on the coffee table because I was hoping he wouldn't notice.

His lips twitched. "Liar." He knelt on the floor, snagging my right calf and setting my foot up on the table, wrapping the compress around it. Then he got up and gave me a kiss. "I'm getting another one; don't move."

I did move though, scooting just far enough down the couch that he had the space by the arm if he wanted it when he got back.

"You moved," he said.

"You gonna tie me to the couch?" I teased.

He snorted and put a hand behind my back to tilt me forward so he could get the compress across my shoulder and back. "You're still on the couch. If you had wandered off anywhere else in this apartment though, well, I can't be held responsible for my actions at that point." He had settled onto the couch in his spot by the arm. He slipped an arm behind me at my waist, reaching around so that his fingers were resting against my thigh.

"Would they involve putting me in a tower? Because you tried that once already, and it didn't work out so well for you."

He twisted, leaning back to look at me. "Yeah? Because it looks like I still got the girl."

I giggled. "You cannot tell me that was your endgame the entire time."

"It absolutely was," he said. "Well, not the way we got thrown together. But yeah, from the moment I saw you come out of those automatic doors, I knew you were the one."

"Oh do not even bullshit me with the love at first sight—"

"Not bullshitting you."

"I think you're hind sighting it with rose colored glasses," I said. "So, what, you showed up at my job the day after coffee because, why? Any excuse to spend time around me?"

"Yeah, pretty much."

"So, you trying to convince me to go on a mission with you—"

"Total lie. I had no idea what I would've done if you had said yes. I didn't have an active mission to take you on at that minute."

"You ass," I said. "What about the whole you'll be a villain spiel?"

"Well, yeah, that actually was my assessment. Good thing I was wrong."

"Eh," I said. "It's a fine line for me."

He nodded, his expression turning serious. "Yeah, sometimes. But you've never gone after someone who didn't deserve it in that moment. Promise me you never will."

Hmm, except that one time I attacked Greg and Virgil. I think it depends on your point of view as to whether Greg and Virgil deserved the level of anger I had toward them at that moment.

"No innocent civilians," I promised. But I can't be held responsible for where I'll go if I lose him. Other than the underworld to drag him back. Even Hades won't stand in my way.

Virgil was right: Greg does have terrible taste in women if we all keep ending up on the dark side. Must be something about opposites attracting. Okay, fine, I only know about the one other one. I haven't asked about anyone else because I don't care.

He settled back against me, kissing my head. "Twenty minutes, and I'll heat those back up."

"We could just get one of those plug-in heating pads."

"No."

"I don't think they're that—"

"Meg, it's not about whether they're a fire hazard."

"Is it because I won't let you rescue me?"

"Yes." He set his other hand on my knee and turned toward me again. I turned my face toward his, and he rested his forehead against mine. "Let me take care of you in the little ways. It makes it easier for me to focus on what we need to do, knowing that when we get home, I can help you that way."

"Okay," I said.

"Okay?"

"Okay." I kissed him. His arm behind me tightened, and he lifted my legs off the coffee table to pull me into his lap. The compress on my ankle fell off, the one at my shoulder sliding down my back.

"Damn it." He started to pull away.

"They can wait," I said. "The bruises aren't going anywhere."

"I don't want them to—"

"I'm pretty sure they're as bad as they're going to get," I said, moving my lips to his neck if he was going to be stubborn about this. "Five minutes."

"That's all you think I'm capable of? Five minutes?"

"I think it's all you're capable of before you start fussing over me again."

"I do not fuss." But I had him where I wanted him, because he was trailing kisses down my neck, onto my unbruised shoulder, his breath tickling against the skin of my collarbone. He had to trade which hand was on my thigh, his fingers splayed against my leg, his thumb brushing back and forth. His other hand was at my back, his fingers working at the band of my bra. He made a frustrated noise. "You're going to have to get the clasp. I'm just going to bend the metal."

I giggled. "What, can't get it undone?"

"No," he growled in my ear. "You want me to admit defeat?"

"I mean, I'm not the one—"

He yanked it apart. "Well, I didn't bend the metal."

"You just tore the stitches, didn't you?" I was half-laughing, half-dismayed, because this wasn't the first one I had lost in this manner. No, I'm not going to tell you the exact number.

"That depends on the stitches you're talking about," he admitted. "But I'm not going to lose to a bra."

I pulled what was left of the bra off and tossed it on the floor. He moved back to pull off his shirt, before he wrapped his arms back around me, one hand in my hair, his lips on mine.

He definitely proved me wrong about the whole five minutes thing.

∞

Flightpath was already at the coffee shop when we arrived.

In the end Greg had decided casual with a way for a quick exit was what he wanted. I thought he chose the coffee shop near our apartment specifically because he knew I would be less likely to murder his dad since I would want to be able to come back to it.

When we got there, Flightpath was standing just off to the side so he wasn't in line, and he smiled, looking relieved when we came in. I was just glad to see he was in street clothes; he'd left the hero outfit at home. Susan, KBC's own star reporter, was still trying to poke her nose into our relationship as entertainment fodder for the masses. She didn't need to know about Greg's dad too.

"Son," he said. "What would you like?"

"Just coffee, for both of us," Greg said.

He waved a hand at us. "Sit, I'll get your orders."

We chose a table by the window, sitting on the side where we would face the door. Greg was in the seat between me and the glass so he could keep an eye on the street outside, one arm slung over my shoulders.

It had taken me a while to realize that when he did that, he was doing it as much for his own comfort as for making sure he had a quick way to pull me against him to shield me.

It wasn't long before Flightpath came over bearing three coffees. He set two down in front of us. "Cream or sugar?" he asked.

"No, thank you," Greg said.

"Sugar's horrible for you," I said, just to be a brat, because Flightpath had snagged one of the sugar packets he had set down on the table. Greg nudged me with his foot. I turned my head to look at him, all innocence. I saw his lips twitch, despite the fact that he was working to keep his face serious.

Flightpath, for his part, ignored my comment, stirring the sugar into his coffee anyway.

There was awkward silence at our table since everyone seemed reluctant to start the conversation. Even though he's quick to forgive, Greg didn't seem inclined to make it easy on his father. Which, fine with me, I'm being silent because I'm trying to follow his lead, snarky sugar comments aside. I assumed Flightpath was silent because he didn't know what to say to his youngest son, the only one of his children with powers.

He finally broke the tension at the table. "Tony told me you had gone freelance. Was your military contract not renewed?"

"I chose not to renew it," Greg said.

"Why?" Flightpath asked. I felt Greg's fingers flex against me.

"We didn't see eye to eye on what were considered acceptable losses on the last mission they assigned me to."

Well, that was the first time Greg had confirmed for me that they had basically told him my death was considered acceptable if it led to Red Eye's. At the time, I had thought he meant just risk in general. No wonder he had been so angry. Loss of civilian lives wasn't okay with Greg at all, complication between us or not.

Flightpath looked considering. "Soldiers give—"

"It wasn't that kind of mission," Greg said.

Flightpath paused. "Civilian lives?"

"Just the one," I said. "But we weren't cool with that."

Flightpath looked surprised. "Tony didn't tell me you two were working together before your current team."

"First mission together," I said cheerfully.

"First mission?" Greg said. "From what I recall someone spent most of the time making the point that she wasn't a hero."

"I'm sorry, who's the one who beat the bad guy?"

"You did, you still—"

"I think that qualifies as hero work. You did say I was the one who saved the world."

"I think you're rewriting history—"

"Am I?" I asked. "Or am I just cherry picking the facts to fit the narrative?"

Greg chuckled.

"You both managed to be up for renewal at the same time?" Flightpath asked doubtfully.

Greg sobered. "No. Vengeance was the civilian."

"This is a relationship built on being rescued?" Flightpath's voice was a mix of concern and judgment.

"No," Greg's tone was short, clipped. "Vengeance made it very clear she didn't need me to rescue her."

"You assisted," I said.

"Hmm," Greg said.

"So, you two met because-?" Flightpath sounded genuinely curious.

"I was up for recruitment duty that go round," Greg said.

"I knew it-!" I started.

"Nope, no. I saw you come out those doors, and that was it. I completely forgot about what I was supposed to be doing." He was smiling at me, the warmth in his eyes. "I lost my footing around you from the start."

"Like that would matter," I said. "You can fly."

Flightpath was watching us. "Now that you're getting married, are you going to retire?"

"No," Greg said, pulling his eyes away from mine.

"Most heroes do," Flightpath said cautiously. "They settle down, start civilian jobs, buy houses."

"Yeah?" Greg said. "Did that work out for you?"

"No," Flightpath said. "It didn't, and your mother didn't understand it."

Greg was silent, I think because he couldn't argue that his mom didn't understand the hero thing always being on.

"I did try," Flightpath said. "We were both very young when we got married and had Tony and Peter, and at that time, I wasn't doing hero work. Then she got pregnant with you when we thought we were long done having any more children. When it was rough on her in a way that the other two hadn't been, I knew you would have at least one power. And what kind of father would I have been without demonstrating the kind of hero you should be?"

"If you were that concerned about being a good father, why did you leave?" Greg asked, and I could hear the anger in his voice.

"Your mother gave me an ultimatum: her or hero work. I chose what I thought was right, but I also didn't realize she would refuse to let me see you."

Greg looked surprised, and I got the feeling his mom had not told him about that.

"Tony and Peter took her side as well. They were young enough still to firmly believe that the sun rose and set on her shoulders but old enough to make their choices clear. Neither of them talked to me until after you had gotten out of high school, and by that point, well, you were on a better path than you had been."

I could feel Greg's arm tensing against me. "You were keeping an eye on me?"

"I heard things through the grapevine, but I couldn't get a clear picture until Tony finally returned my phone calls."

Greg grunted. "I'm sure that picture was extremely unbiased."

"I think your brother is worried that you will slide."

"Slide into what?" And there was warning in Greg's tone. "Because I am well aware of what Tony thinks of me."

"Another bad crowd," Flightpath said.

"I think I'm safe from bad crowds at this point," Greg said.

Flightpath was silent for a long moment. "I believe Tony feels somewhat responsible for you and your high school experience not being what it should have been. I think he's trying to make up for that."

"Well, he can stop," Greg said. "I already have someone who's keeping me on the straight and narrow."

Flightpath eyed me. "Are you sure?"

I snorted. "He doesn't mean me. I'm a bad influence."

Greg laughed and kissed my head. "You're a better influence than you think."

I knew who he meant. It wasn't Virgil, although he certainly helped keep Greg steady. It was the ghosts of whoever haunted him, either from the hard lesson he got, or the people he wasn't in time to save. Maybe both. Still though.

"I'm a horrible influence," I said. "I believe the word you've used is incorrigible."

"That is completely unrelated—" Greg said.

"Is it though?" I said, smirking at him. "Because I'm pretty sure you've unashamedly taken advantage of the benefit of me being incorrigible in the first place."

"Hmm," Greg said, because I had him caught, and he knew it. "Needs must."

Flightpath's phone pinged, and he pulled it out of his pocket, to check the message. He frowned, and stood. "I'm sorry, I have to handle this. I would like, if you are amenable, to be able to get coffee with you again. With or without Vengeance."

"Okay," Greg said.

"I can call you to set it up?"

"Yes."

Flightpath nodded, relief on his face again. "I will speak to you about it later then. Vengeance, it was nice to meet you in a less official capacity." He went out the door and took off.

Greg was frowning at his coffee cup. "What?" I asked him.

"Is it like that with me?" he asked.

"Is what like that with you?"

"The thing where—" he waved a hand at Flightpath's seat, "do I make you feel slighted?"

"No," I said.

"No?"

"No. You always take me with you."

"Like you would let me do anything else," he said, but his mood seemed to have lifted.

"Hmm," I said, and because I'm a mood killer, "are you going to talk to your mom?"

He scrubbed at his face. "I don't think I'm ready for that conversation." He stood, grabbing the trash off the table. "Come on, Virgil's going to want us back before any more gods or snakes show up."

CHAPTER ELEVEN

Virgil had wanted us back. He was in the lab, having already collected Ranger and Maniac, and was hanging blueprints up on the wall. Once they were up there, he stepped back.

The sewer system for a city this size is massive, a labyrinth of tunnels crisscrossing their way under the city and around the subway system.

"Seriously," Ranger said. "I don't understand how this city stays up to start with."

Virgil had his hand on his chin. "There are sections I think we can discount as being too small for a monster the size of that Gorgon."

"Snakes are pretty flexible," Ranger said. "I'm not sure we can discount anything."

"An astute point," Virgil said. "Well, we better hope he prefers a large cavern-like space for nesting. We'll check those first, and fortunately, there are only five. It's the amount of system we have to cross through to get to them first that has me concerned. We can't afford to get ambushed."

"What are we doing about lights down there?" Greg asked.

"Probably headlamps," Virgil said. "Night vision won't

work; it's going to be too dark." He was pinching the bridge of his nose.

"Why not just torches?" Maniac asked. "Wouldn't that have been what they used in the old tales?"

"Some of us want our hands free for weapons," Ranger said.

"You trading the bat out?" I asked.

"Temporarily," he said, grinning at me.

Virgil had summoned himself a highlighter from somewhere and was tracing a path to the first of the cavern-like areas. "What I want to do is set up observation in each of these spots. With the time it's going to take to get there and back, we're going to have to delve into the sewers on more than one trip."

"That's risky," Greg said.

"Not as risky as just wandering around down there until we run into the thing."

"My snack stash is not equipped for that," Maniac said.

I giggled. "We'll top it off after each trip."

"If you could take this seriously, please," Virgil said. "I don't know that we need to be taking the entire team down each time if all we're doing is recon."

Maniac, Ranger, Greg and I all protested at the same.

"No, that's—"

"I am not staying—"

"What if you—"

"Enough!" Virgil said. "Please, one at a time. Greg, as the only level-headed one—"

"He is not—" Ranger started. I got the feeling I might agree with whatever Ranger was about to say.

"I know exactly what he is," Virgil said. "He is level-headed enough for this. Greg, your opinion."

"Who did you want to take with you?" Greg asked. "Before we get into arguments about who is or isn't going."

"How come you assume Virgil is going?" Ranger asked.

"Because he's the one who knows how to set up the

cameras," Greg crossed his arms. "So if we're setting up for recon, he has to go."

Ranger just grunted.

"Greg, Ranger, you're on the recon team," Virgil said.

"Excuse me?" Maniac and I said at the same time.

"I don't see a problem with this," Ranger said.

"You wouldn't," I said. "Why are Maniac and I the ones getting left behind for this? I'm the—"

"Do not try and pull the god card with me," Virgil said. "Because I'm holding the aces."

"That is not what I was going to say," I said, offended. "I was going to say I'm the one with the most information about what we're facing." And maybe I was going to use the god card if that didn't work.

"And you kindly already shared that information with the class," Virgil said. I scowled at him. "Now, the reason for leaving you behind is that one, your skills aren't needed for this kind of recon. We don't need to question anyone, and your physical vulnerability means if we end up engaging, someone will be hamstrung to keep you protected in an ambush."

"I could literally just scare it off."

"How well did that work for you in the park?"

I glared at him, my arms crossed, and muttered.

"What's that?" Virgil asked. "Can't hear you."

"Not well," I said.

"Thank you. I do promise that once we get down to the actual business of ending it, you will be included on that operation."

"Still haven't explained why I get to cool my heels up here," Maniac said.

"Because you'll be on 'make sure Meg doesn't do anything stupid' duty."

"I do not need a babysitter!" I said.

"Yeah, I think she can handle herself," Maniac said, "so I'm not taking that job."

"We have gods popping into our apartment and

wandering the city streets. I don't want you left here alone while the rest of us are occupied."

"Then we should just all go," I said.

"No," Virgil said. "If I could, I would go alone, but I need at least one person guarding my back while I'm getting these things set up. Taking Ranger and Greg is going to be the most economical."

"Why not just one of us?" Ranger asked. "Not that I'm arguing about going."

"Greg can ensure a quick exit for us. You can slow it if we get ambushed, giving us time for the quick exit."

"You're going to expect me to just be cool with attack dog flying us out of there?"

"You would rather be snake food?" Virgil asked.

"If it turns me to stone, is it really going to be trying to eat me?"

"Relax," Greg said. "You won't hit anything on the way out."

"Yeah? Am I going to hit something like the ground after that point?"

"Worried I'll drop you?"

"No," Ranger said. "More like worried you'll throw me. I don't trust you that far."

Virgil cleared his throat. "We seem to have reached the end of any progress we can make with this discussion. So, if we could, I need time to gather the supplies we'll need and then the *three* of us will head out after lunch. I want to be done with the first camera installation before dark if possible."

Maniac's phone pinged, and she pulled it out. When she looked at the message, her eyes widened. "Oh, that's not good."

"What?" Virgil's voice was sharp.

"Grenadier says he can see me."

"He what?" Greg said. "Why are you even still in contact with him if you-?"

"I'm not," she snapped. "I keep changing numbers, and

he keeps getting it."

"Who's Grenadier? And see you how?" I asked. In the apartment Virgil had set up for the lab, he had blocked all the windows. No one should be able to see in.

"Villain I used to know, and I don't–" but she stopped, her mouth in an O of surprise. "Oh fuck, get down!"

Greg tackled me, and then the side of the building blew up.

It blasted inward, bricks, drywall, huge splinters of wood from the studs, shards of glass flying at us. The pieces had frozen, vibrating in the air, both Virgil and Ranger with their hands up, palms out. Maniac was crouched, her back to the blast behind them.

"Can you reverse it?" Virgil was asking.

"No, the blast will just keep going off every time I release it. We need to go." Ranger nudged Maniac with the back of his foot. "Get up and run." He didn't have to tell her twice; she surged up and out, headed for the door. Greg scooped me up off the floor from where he had thrown himself on top of me to shield me from the explosion, charging after Maniac for the stairwell. She went down; Greg went up.

"Wait!" I said.

"She can handle herself," Greg said. "I'm getting us into the air so we can spot him." He slammed the door to the roof open. Well, more like he went straight through it with his shoulder. I heard the metallic clang of it as it bent and then the screech when the hinges tore and the lock broke.

"The landlord is going to be pissed," I said and then gave a yelp of surprise when Greg launched us straight up.

He adjusted me, shifting me around, his arm still wrapped up under me, so I was cradled with my back against his chest, sitting on his forearm. He kept his other arm wrapped around my waist. "Do you see anyone on the rooftops?"

I was looking around, trying not to panic. He had me; I was secure, but I wasn't seeing any movement on any of the roofs below us. "No," I said. "Did he already run?"

"He would be stupid not to," Greg said. He was drifting us over the side the lab was on, looking down, his chin on my shoulder. "I'm trying to figure out where he could come out from."

"Wouldn't he have had to have a clear view of what he's shooting at?" I asked.

"No," Greg growled. "He could've been on any side of the building; he can steer those fucking things."

"Like heat-seeking missiles?"

"Yeah. He's the one who hit me with the rocket launcher."

There was a loud, PHOMPF sound below us and then the clatter of falling wood, shattered glass. "Ranger and Virgil must've let go of the blast itself," Greg said.

"I hope they're okay," I said, trying to lean forward to look down. "What does this asshole look like?"

Greg was making that strangled noise again. "Meg, lean back."

"Why? You're not going to drop me."

He was grinding his teeth. "No, but——"

"So, let me look."

He sighed, loosened his grip just a bit, so I could lean forward against his arm, Looking at the people, the activity on the street. There were already sirens going in the distance, so at least our neighbors had called in the explosion rather than just ignoring it. But that wasn't my main concern. I was looking for someone carrying a rocket launcher, or a case that could fit one, but then I thought about it.

"If he can steer them, does he need a way to launch them in the first place?"

"No."

"What does he look like?" I repeated.

"Red hair, freckles. Actually, he reminds me of that ventriloquist dummy from those kid's books."

"What, *Goosebumps*?"

"Yeah, those."

"He wear anything that would make him easier to pick out?"

"I think you already know the answer to that." Which meant no, he didn't. Unlike heroes, villains don't want to stand out from the crowd.

There were too many people on the street, and I wasn't spotting anyone with red hair. "I think we've missed him."

"Or he's hiding in one of the buildings until we give up," Greg said.

"We going to do a building-by-building search?"

"No," Greg said, landing us back on the roof, "but now we have to move."

"Ranger can just reverse—"

"I know what Ranger can do. We still have to move; he's going to be back."

I frowned, thinking. "Do you want me to see if Ares will track him down for us?"

"No. I don't want you beholden to any of them for some sort of favor or something."

"You and Virgil been doing some reading?" I asked.

"Maybe," Greg said. "I don't know how they operate, and that puts me at a disadvantage if we have to bargain with them."

"Too bad you-know-who doesn't still owe me," I muttered.

"Absolutely under no circumstances do you strike any kind of bargain with him."

I twisted as much as I could to face him because he still hadn't set me down. "I won't." Well, to be honest, if we had to make a bargain with Bacchus, we were already super screwed on whatever we were facing, so he would be beyond my last choice. I would rather strike a deal with Hera.

"Good," he said, his arms tightening against me. Then he set me down. "Come on, we need to check on the others."

We went through the remnants of the door and down the stairs to our hall. The hallway was full of smoke still, some of it slowly drifting back out the door to the lab. The sprinklers of the fire protection system were already on, soaking the hallway and knocking more smoke out of the air. Greg and I stayed back in the stairwell, and when we heard footsteps coming up from below us, he immediately moved in front of me.

It was only Ranger, Virgil and Maniac. Virgil strode past us into what was left of his lab and swore. "My fucking cameras!" He came back into the stairwell dripping wet. "Ranger, can you reverse this?"

Ranger shook his head. "No, I'm going to end up reversing the explosion too unless we can pick out all the pieces first."

That made me think. "What did you do about the bullet in my chest?"

"Virgil got it out first."

Maniac was eyeing me. "Bullet?"

"I died once," I said.

"Guess you got better."

Greg was making that strangled sound and grinding his teeth at the same time. "It wouldn't matter if we can reverse it. They've got fire trucks and ambulances on the way already. And then everyone is going to know where we've been holing up. We have to move, and we have to do it now."

Virgil swore again. "Okay, Maniac, Greg, Meg, you're in the Cobra with me. Ranger follow on your bike."

"The compound?" Ranger asked.

"No," Virgil said. "Right now, we're just getting off site. I don't want to end up leading anyone to our safe house." He turned, heading down the stairs, and the rest of us followed.

∞

Virgil parked the Cobra in an alley in a derelict, warehouse district part of town. Ranger pulled his bike up next to the driver side window and then stared at Virgil until Virgil rolled the window down.

"Seriously?" he said. "We're going to camp out here?"

"Yes," Virgil said. "These warehouses are abandoned, so we won't have to worry about civilians when Grenadier comes calling again."

Maniac and I were leaning forward to look out the window, since we were the ones who had gotten squished into the backseat. Virgil turned to look at us. "Do you mind?"

Greg scrubbed at his face. "Okay, what do you need a temporary base of operations to have? Ranger and I can go looking for one that matches it."

Virgil had leaned back, classic thinking pose, one arm across his chest, the other hand at his chin. "They're all going to be pretty much the same. I do want to park the Cobra and bike inside, so they're not left on the street for any yahoo to borrow. I don't need them scratching up the paint."

"So centrally located?" Greg asked. "Because out here we might run into people who have different reasons for hiding."

"Which is exactly why I don't want the Cobra in plain view. Retrieving my property on top of everything else doesn't need to be on the to do list. Find one that isn't occupied over by the harbor side. Being near the water might be prudent."

"On it," Greg said, getting out of the car. "Ranger you coming?"

Ranger jerked his head, revved the engine of his bike and took off. Greg followed, airborne only a few seconds later.

Virgil was pinching the bridge of his nose. "Maniac, is there anyone else you're aware of who's been actively pursuing you?"

"They're all pursuing me," she said. "It just depends on whether chasing me fits into their current projects."

"That answer is singularly unhelpful," Virgil said. "Have you heard from any of the others that would tell you they're aware of where you are?"

"Well now that Grenadier knows where I am, they

probably all do."

"I thought you guys didn't really talk to each other," I said.

Maniac snorted. "We don't, except for this shit." She paused, thought about it. "Well, sometimes we check in to make sure we're not interfering in whatever someone else is up to. Because otherwise someone dies when we run afoul of each other's plans."

"Didn't think you would care about that either," I muttered.

"We don't. Well, okay, we don't when we're confident we're not the one who's going to die."

I straightened up. "Virgil, could we give them a new target to worry about?"

He turned to look at us, twisted in his seat. "What are you thinking?"

"Tell them about Mirage."

Maniac was looking between the two of us. "Mirage is dead. Aren't you the one who killed him?"

"Mirage used Meg to fake his own death," Virgil said.

"No way!" Maniac said. "Could we do that for me?"

"How are you supposed to keep your cover from getting blown?" Virgil said. "You're doing hero work; you'd have to completely retire. And you can't do that until the Gorgon is dead."

Maniac sat back. "Damn. No, I don't want to retire anyway."

"So?" I said. "Let's give them a different target to worry about at least until we've got the giant snake problem solved."

"That doesn't seem like a fair way to repay him for his help against Red Eye," Virgil said.

I suppressed a shudder. "We blackmailed him into helping in the first place. I doubt he expects us to keep this a secret forever. He's probably already run somewhere new."

Virgil sighed. "You have a point. It would be stupid of him not to move his base of operations. He was willing to trust me not to expose him, but you and Greg not so much."

I snorted. "Greg wouldn't."

"No, he wouldn't," Virgil agreed. "Useful ally and all that. Regardless of either of your personal feelings on him."

"That's great," Maniac said, "really great. Which move are we making? Because I don't feel like dying any time soon regardless of however they brought you back."

"We need to discuss it as a group," Virgil said.

"Why?" I asked. "We have a plan, and we know which number Grenadier is contacting Maniac from. We can just text him right back."

"No," Virgil said. "We will do no such thing. I am not exposing Mirage without including Greg in this."

"Excuse me, but I'm—"

"I know what you are," Virgil said, pointing a finger at me, "and you are still looking for vengeance against him, and it's a petty reason. You are going to have to let it go because he could prove useful in the future if Greg and Ranger are against this plan. Because I am."

"It would buy us time—" I started to argue.

"Not enough time," Virgil said. "They may just decide to divide their attention or even double their efforts against Maniac and take Mirage down afterwards. There are too many variables and no guarantees with your plan."

I glared at him.

"Glare at me all you want," Virgil said. "I'm right and you know it."

"Oh, so, we're voting on it?" Maniac said.

"It would appear we will be," Virgil said.

"Great. I vote no."

"What?!" I protested. "You're going to take Virgil's side in this?"

"I'm not a snitch," she said.

I muttered, crossing my arms. "Fine, I'll just be wrong over here by myself."

"You do that," she said.

Greg was swinging the car door open, poking his head in to look at me. "Wrong by yourself on what?"

"Meg wanted to tell Grenadier about Mirage to get him off Maniac's back until we can resolve the Gorgon problem," Virgil told him.

"Hmm," Greg said. "Yeah, unless Ranger takes your side on that one, you're on your own."

"Some fiancé you are," I said.

"We owe him," Greg said.

"Yeah, we owe him a trip to the morgue," I argued.

Maniac eyed me. "Are you sure you're not the villain type?"

Greg chuckled. "Meg's borderline."

"When you're all done ganging up on me and my hero or villain status, I believe you were supposed to be finding Virgil a hidey hole for his car," I said.

Greg climbed into the car, settling in the seat. "Yeah, pull a left out of the alley. We're going to go down about ten warehouses. There's a nice empty one down there; I left the locks alone. There weren't any heartbeats other than mice, so I figured you would want to pick the padlocks rather than have to replace them."

"Where's Ranger?" I asked.

Greg shrugged. "I'll find him once Virgil's got the car parked."

"What's the lettering on the warehouse?" Virgil asked.

"G54," Greg said.

"Go find Ranger now. I don't like us being separated for too long."

Greg sighed but heaved himself back out of the car, shut the door, and took off.

Virgil started the car, pulled out of the alley and down the strip, leaning over the steering wheel as he counted down the warehouses. He pulled up to a rolling door, paused and looked at us. "I want everyone out of the car so we can move quickly if anything shows up." He put the car in park and climbed out. Maniac and I followed.

Being exposed like this made my shoulders itch. Maniac and I were both looking around, but the strip was empty. We were currently the only sign of life. Virgil was hunched over the padlock at the bottom of the door. I heard it click as it released. He stowed the lock in his pocket and then started to straighten up as he pushed the door up its tracks. It squealed and then stuck.

"Fuck," he said. "Meg, Maniac, come hold it up so it doesn't drop on me. I need to get under it and see why it's blocked."

We each grabbed a side of the door, and Virgil let go, lying down on his back and sliding under it, his chest positioned beneath it. "Don't drop it," he reminded us.

"Would you die?" Maniac asked.

"No, but it would hurt," Virgil said. There was the screech of metal on metal, and then the door yanked up out of our grasps.

"Shit! Warn a person next time," Maniac yelped.

Virgil was standing, the door having rolled all the way back. "Get inside; I'll move the car."

"Not even an apology," Maniac muttered as we headed into the warehouse. It was an empty, cavernous room. A small shed-like space sat in the far corner from us. There was an exterior door in the wall to our right that probably led into the alley beside the building. There were no walkways, only rafters for the metal roof above us. Hanging lights were positioned between them, long windows spaced out at the top, but I didn't see a way for anyone to access them to start with.

Maniac tried the light switch next to the door. Nothing happened.

"No electricity?" I asked.

"Looks like it," she said. We both moved out of the way, and Virgil drove the Cobra in, the rumble of the engine echoing off the walls and concrete floor. He took the opportunity to turn it around so that it faced out before he shut the car off.

The growl of a different engine, and then Ranger's bike came into view. He steered in and was followed by Greg.

"Good, we're all here," Virgil said. The garage-like door squealed again as it rolled shut.

The warehouse got a lot darker without any of the light that had been spilling in from that door. Virgil pulled out his phone. "Okay, we need to make a list. Other than food and water, what do we need?"

"There's no electricity," I told him.

"Not worried about that. Maniac can just char the food."

She snorted. "I am not your personal oven and stove."

"Sleeping bags," Ranger said.

"Air mattresses preferably," Greg said.

"You got a problem with sleeping on the ground?" Ranger asked.

"I don't do camping," I said.

"This doesn't qualify as camping," Ranger said, "and I already knew you didn't want to do camping. Still think you and attack dog should give it a try."

"Bears," I reminded him.

Greg was scrubbing his face. "Can we argue about what qualifies as camping or if it will even happen after our current crisis is averted?"

"Air mattresses, pillows and bedding," Virgil said, "although I would prefer things we can abandon that can still be used by anyone not villain-related who comes across it."

"Sleeping bags," Greg said. "We'll just have to deal with being on the concrete."

"No, no, we're going to want cots at least," Ranger said. "That concrete is going to suck out our body heat."

"It's summer," I said.

"Yeah? You want to sleep cold?"

"Enough!" Virgil said. "I do not have the patience for quibbling right now. We have complications we did not need going on. We need nonperishables, bottled water, cots and sleeping bags."

"Chairs?" Greg asked.

"We can just sit on the cots," Ranger said. "Grab at least five, maybe six, just in case. We should try to keep our items as minimal as possible though."

"Clothes," I said. "We don't have any. They're all back at the apartments."

"Did you remember your suit?" Virgil asked.

"No," I said. "I wasn't wearing it for coffee, so it's back home." I could see how he might have missed it; I was wearing Greg's sweatshirt anyway.

It was comfy, and it smelled like him. Although it was a little holey at that point.

Virgil sighed. "I'm not going to be able to get another one of those quickly. Okay, we need to concentrate on supplies. At some point one of us is going to need to risk getting back into the apartments to retrieve anything there that we need. Like the swords."

"What about your cameras?" Greg asked. "We can't set up for observation until you get new ones, can we?"

"No," Virgil said. "I need everything: cameras, monitors, receivers, et cetera. I did not need this fucking monkey wrench."

Virgil must be really, really pissed right now.

If I mentioned asking Ares for help, would Virgil side with Greg or with me on the bargaining bit?

"Okay," Greg said. "Who's going to REI?"

"You are," Virgil said. "You're the only one who can carry all that without needing a vehicle."

"Who's going for the food and things?"

"Also you," Virgil said. "Two trips, that's it. I don't want us exposed any more than necessary. You're going to be the hardest to trace the path of."

"Noted," Greg said. "I'm going. The sooner we're set up as well as we can be the better." He gave me a kiss and headed for the door.

"Watch yourself," I said.

"Always," he said, shooting me a smile as he lifted the door so he could step under it. Then he was gone, the door firmly back on the ground.

With Greg gone, I turned to Virgil. "Ares," I said.

"What about Ares?"

"Would it be worth bargaining with him to track Grenadier down for us?"

He looked like he was about to protest, then paused, back to thoughtful. "But would he do it in the first place?"

"He seems to like me."

"He's also—" Virgil paused again, his eyes narrowed. "Greg already asked you not to bargain with them, didn't he?"

"Just the one specific one." A half-lie, since Greg didn't want me stuck owing any of them anything. "I don't see what would be wrong with asking what the price would be."

"I think this is another discussion that we all need to be present for," Virgil said, "but yes, finding out the cost for assistance is not a bad idea."

"I'm not sure I like this plan," Ranger said.

"We don't have to agree on it," I said.

"Why don't—" Maniac said, "and stick with me here, because it's a crazy plan— why don't we call the other *hero* who has already shown up and helped us out before?"

I started to open my mouth to argue but then shut it because I hadn't even considered Flightpath as a possibility. Personal history aside, Greg would probably be much more comfortable working with his dad than a god of questionable motives.

"I like that idea," Ranger said.

"You just going to take everyone else's side?" I asked, grumpy because I was losing all the arguments.

"I'm going to take everyone else's side when you're trying to rush into the worst possible plan because you're in too much of a hurry to think it through, yeah."

"Are we done?" Virgil said. "I would prefer to save bargaining with the gods as a last resort. We will talk to Greg when he gets back between errands, since it's his father we would be dealing with."

I scowled and sat down on the floor. "You know he's going to pick that option over any other."

"Yes, he is. I would still like to make sure he's aware he has a choice before we move ahead."

"Like you wouldn't steer him into whatever you want to do anyway," I said.

"Greg is unfortunate that he has gotten stuck with the two of us, pot."

I grinned at him. "Kettle."

Ranger's face was doing the shadowed look again, and he turned his head, so he was looking at the floor and not at me, but then he turned back to Virgil. "What can this Grenadier guy do? Other than blow buildings up."

"Greg said he can steer the missiles?" I said.

"He can steer missiles?" Ranger asked.

"Grenades. He can steer rocket-powered grenades. Hence the name," Virgil said.

"Can he steer anything larger than that?" Ranger asked. "Because I don't want to be on the business end of something nuclear."

"To my knowledge, no. He cannot steer anything that already has a guidance system."

"So, is he telekinetic?" I asked.

"No," Virgil said. "Too specialized. His power lends itself to explosives only."

"I don't see how that's any better," Ranger said. "How many grenades can he steer at once? Can he do it with TNT? What are we talking about in terms of the amount he can get to blow up at once?"

"He can't just steer them through the air indefinitely," Maniac said. "He's got to carry them on him until he's close to his target. And it has to be something rocket powered, not just straight explosives."

"So, he can't just hit us from across the city," Ranger said.

"No," Maniac said. "He has to see us, essentially."

"About that," I said. "How could he see us?"

"He can see heat signatures," Maniac said.

Virgil started. "He can?"

"Yeah. He doesn't really advertise it, but he yelled at me once because my flames were fucking up his ability to see. So I was yelling at him that his project was not my problem—"

Virgil waved off the rest of her comment. "But he can see heat signatures in an occupied building?"

"Yes."

Virgil swore. "So if he followed us, he can pick out which warehouse we're in?"

"He would have to take an educated guess based on the number of signatures in the warehouse itself, but yeah."

Virgil was pinching the bridge of his nose, his fingers rubbing his eyes. "We're going to have to hope he didn't follow us here, and we'll have to take shifts for sleeping and keeping watch. Meg, get off the floor, we can't afford to be anything but ready to run."

I stood up, my shoulders and back tense now.

I don't want to get blown up any more than I want to get shot. I mean, yeah, I got shot the one time, but let's not repeat that experience.

"Why don't we just trap him?" I asked.

"I would love to do that," Virgil said. "Because we will have to take him out, and quickly so we can get back to the much more urgent issue at hand. The problem being that he will be able to see where we all are, gathered together or if we're off in separate teams."

"Safety in numbers would work better," Maniac said, "but then we would be endangering other people and someone on this team has an issue with that."

"We all have an issue with that," Ranger said pointedly.

"At least, we better."

"Well good for you never having to compromise your morals for the sake of the mission," Maniac said. "Sometimes you need to be practical."

"I thought you had a problem with the heroes who don't watch out for civilians," I said.

"I have a problem with heroes who lie about it," Maniac said. "They don't care. They let people die and then act like nothing happened. Same as the villains. At least when I'm talking about hiding out in a crowd, I'm admitting there's a problem with it even if it's the smart choice."

"But not a choice we can make," Virgil said. "Maniac, how long can you hold the flames in place? Can we set up multiple spots to mislead him into thinking there are more people than there are?"

Maniac snorted. "No, I can't shape it and the signature would look wrong anyway. And I definitely can't just hold it there forever."

Virgil was thinking again. "We're going to want to keep moving in that case. Limit the likelihood that he tracks us down before we're ready to take him on. One surprise explosion was one too many."

The door squealed as it lifted up, and we all swung to face it, Ranger having planted himself next to me while the whispers settled against my shoulders.

"It's just me," Greg said, his foot pushing through six flat, rectangular boxes. Then he lifted the gate higher, ducking under it and dropped several tightly rolled sleeping bags onto the floor, before rolling the door back down. The whispers faded.

"Good," Virgil said. "Maniac thinks we should call Flightpath for help tracking Grenadier down."

Greg grunted, as he lifted the topmost box, ripping the cardboard open. "That's not a bad idea."

Virgil waited, and after a moment of silence, Greg looked up from the box and sighed. "Now?"

"Yes, now."

Greg set the box down, pulled his phone out, and typed out a text. "There. Now he's aware, but he bailed on coffee pretty quick, so he might be busy."

CHAPTER TWELVE

Eventually, after a whole lot of discussion, side tracking, quibbling and trying what was left of Virgil's patience, we came to the agreement that we were going for teams of two, two and one. Greg would be on his own, after much heated arguing from me, but I got overruled because of the whole compulsion thing, Ranger and me, and then Virgil and Maniac. The plan was to keep the warehouse as our base of operations while we searched Grenadier out. Virgil had asked Maniac if Grenadier would show up for an invitation to try and take her down, and she had laughed, so we took that as a no.

By the time we got done going around in circles and Greg had come back with food and water, it was getting dark.

Greg took first watch, Ranger volunteered for second, and Virgil said he was taking third because he would be awake anyway. When Maniac and I tried to argue that we were capable of taking a watch, Virgil told us we would be trading off nights, so the two of us were on the roster for tomorrow.

I was both mollified and mad about it. What? You want to be up in the middle of the night trying to listen for someone who can just lob RPGs without you even being aware he's there? Didn't think so. We just didn't want to be excluded.

Greg had set up on the roof outside, and I heard the way the metal echoed when he landed. The rest of us had already gone to bed, mostly because Virgil told us we might as well get some rest.

I woke up some point after Greg and Ranger had traded out because Greg had one hand resting on my back when I opened my eyes.

I could smell brine in the air, and the memory of who it preceded made us wary. The whispers were tugging at me, the sound of our name floating on the wind.

I slid out from under Greg's hand and off the cot and padded quietly to the door out. Ranger was at the corner hidden in the shadows of the alley, watching the main strip, his back to me. I was faced with a choice: tell Ranger what I could sense or walk away before he noticed me.

I went down the alley away from him, cutting up behind the building, headed for the harbor. The whispers curled against me, the figures furling down the metal walls, shadows flowing along the ground, pooled at my feet when we stopped at the water's edge.

Here, the banks of the harbor were concrete retaining walls, rising at a minimum a good five feet above the water's surface. I stood as close to where it dropped as possible, my toes at the edge of the pavement.

Even here, away from the bustling city center, you can't really see the stars. The light pollution from all the buildings flanking the harbor banks is too much. I could see the lights reflecting off the water's surface and hear the slap of the waves against the cement. The smell of salt was so strong, but there was no one here but the whispers, the figures, the shadows and me.

The water below us swirled.

"Meg!"

I started, turning, and Ranger was striding up to me, the expression on his face stern. "What are you doing out here?" he asked. If anything his tone of voice was even more serious.

"You can't be doing midnight wanderings just because you can't sleep."

"I thought…" I said, turning back to look down at the water, but there was nothing there to see other than the rippling waves. The whispers were pressing on my ears; something was here, and we needed to be cautious.

"You need to go back inside," Ranger said, and I was turning to face him when I saw the flame in the air. Without thinking, I grabbed his jacket and yanked us both over the bank's edge.

There was a BOOM above us, flames and smoke, and then we hit the water as the shockwave from the explosion hit us.

That's now an experience I don't want to repeat either.

Ranger's body slammed into mine, and then the water hit my back, so I was sandwiched between the two forces. The waves closed over my head. I could feel Ranger wrap an arm around my back and then the pull as he fought us to the surface.

Our heads popped up, and immediately I got slapped in the face by another wave while I was trying to take a breath. I choked, coughing and gasping.

"Fuck," he said, trying to help me stay up.

I never learned to swim. As a kid, I was scared of what was in the water because the whispers refused to go in it. Once I was old enough to overcome that fear, there was high school, and track and the party, and then I just never bothered.

I did not think the dodge the explosion move through.

The whispers were howling, the figures swirling, the shadows stretched out along the surface of the waves, trying to rise above them.

"Greg!" Ranger was bellowing. But there were more explosions, and I didn't know how quickly Greg would be able to locate us among all the noise. Ranger flipped me around, so his arms were under mine, holding my head above water. "GREG!" he yelled again.

Something wound around my leg. "Let go!" I gasped at Ranger, trying to warn him. I had a bad feeling about this, and he needed to get away.

"I'm not—" Ranger started to protest, and then I was jerked back under the water, and because he was holding on to me, he went under too.

He slipped away from me. Or I slipped away from him. The something that had me had wound around my arms and torso now, and then my body had hit the bottom of the harbor, dragging along through the silt and sand. If it hadn't already been dark down there, it would've been impossible to see with all the debris being kicked up.

The whispers, figures and shadows had had no choice but to go under with me. I could hear the whispers shrieking, the sound muffled and gargling, which was an odd thing for me to notice when my lungs were burning and I was desperate for air. You would think I would be more concerned about not drowning.

Whatever it was that had a hold of me let go. I floated up, hanging in the water, too high to touch the bottom of the river, too far from the surface for the sudden freedom to be of any use. I wouldn't be able to struggle up there on my own.

I could feel a hand gripping my upper arm, pulling me back down to the harbor floor, then a pair of fingers pinching my nose, and I tried to rear back from it, but someone's mouth was on mine forcing air into my lungs.

Instinctively I squirmed, trying to get away, regardless of the lifesaving they were gifting because those were most definitely not Greg's lips on mine. But their grip only tightened, and whoever it was began moving us through the water, almost languidly.

That made me panic, desperately twisting, trying to wrench free. With the water rushing past us it felt like they weren't going up, but like they were going to the side. I could feel my feet trailing along the riverbed. I thrashed, kicking out at them, the whispers screaming in my ears, but their arms had wrapped around me, and they sped up, and the whispers were ignoring my calls for help. Or they couldn't help.

The hands were on my face again, and I wrenched my head away, gasping in water instead of the air they offered.

If I lived through this, I needed to work on my survival instincts.

∞

When I woke up, I was looking at the sky. I had been out long enough that the sun was up, a ball of light at its zenith. It hurt to breathe, like my lungs and throat had been scraped raw. I could feel wet sand under my hands, waves brushing up my legs, my clothes still soaked. With a groan I sat up, my hair clinging to my neck and shoulders, dripping.

I could smell the brine in the air, so I turned my head. My apparent "rescuer" was sitting next to me, his dark hair also wet, straggling and clinging to the tanned skin of his neck and face. He met my gaze with eyes the dark green of the raging sea.

Poseidon was naked.

I went bright red and scrambled away from him, stumbling, and falling to my knees only a few feet away. Apparently, I was going to need more than several hours of unconsciousness to recover from nearly drowning. I did manage to get myself turned around so I could keep an eye on where he was in relation to me.

He hadn't moved. He just watched me, the silence between us stretching. Between it and the nudity I was pretty sure my muscles were going to tear from how tense I was.

I cleared my throat because I couldn't stand the staring contest any longer. "Do you think you could get dressed?"

"No," he said.

I was trying to think of a way not to be rude about telling him to put on some damn clothes. I went for the circumspect route. "Why not?"

"They'll just rot," he said. "And they drag in the water. They hamper my movements." He turned his face back toward the water.

Since he didn't seem interested in coming after me, I took the opportunity to look around. We were near the harbor, still surrounded by the city. He must have brought me ashore one of the little islands that dot the river traveling inland.

Of course, one of them features in an urban legend about an escaped serial killer with a hook for a hand, so I'm not sure if this situation is an improvement over Grenadier.

When he still didn't move, I stood up, intending to walk around the shoreline until I found a boat out on the river and could get their attention to come pick me up. I didn't have my phone on me; it was back in the warehouse with everyone else. Well, if they were even still there. And it wouldn't matter if I had it on me anyway because the water would've ruined it.

"You owe me a debt," he said.

"Do I?" I asked. "I don't recall agreeing to any favors."

"You do. Although the favor was hard to bestow upon you."

"What exactly do you think I owe you for?"

He somehow managed to look down his nose at me, even though I was standing, and he was still sitting. "I could've left you to drown. Your anchor is fragile. Unusually so. I was not expecting that."

"Did you try to drown me in the first place? Because I feel like that means any debt would be null and void."

"The debt stands," he said. "However it was incurred to start with."

I could see I was about to argue a god in circles, and eventually he was going to get angry because although it was one of his monsters that grabbed me, he would've expected me to get my own ass out of the situation or die. As far as he was concerned, I owed him for his interference.

"Great," I said. "What exactly do I owe?"

He shrugged. "When I decide what I want, I'll come to

you."

"Like, inland? Because I live in an apartment." Oh wait, technically I don't have my apartment right now. Whatever, he's a god. He can figure it out.

"Wherever the sea is, I can reach you from it."

I wasn't sure if I wanted to ask him to clarify that statement because from what I remembered, being landlocked wasn't going to help me avoid him.

Well, in for a penny in for a pound. "Since I already owe you, want to do me another favor, or two?"

"A bargain?"

"Yeah, let's just add it to my tab."

He shifted to face me, and I ducked my head to the side, cheeks burning to stare at the ground. Because I was so busy trying to avoid looking at him, I didn't notice his approach until he was next to me. I kept my eyes trained on the sand and the water.

"Ask what you will of me, and I will tell you my price," he said.

"Keep Zeus away from me." If I'm going in, I'm going all in.

He clucked his tongue. "You ask too much. That I cannot, and would not, do."

Damn it.

"You said you had a second favor?" he asked.

"Where's the Gorgon hiding?"

"Where he's always hidden, in a cavern by the sea. Two debts: one small, one large. When I have need of you, I'll call."

Then he was gone, foaming away into the waves lapping at the shore.

"Thought you were going to tell me the price," I muttered.

Now I had to figure out how to get back to the main shore. The side of the island I was on, facing the length of the river, didn't have any boats that I could see. Buildings on the banks across rose to the left and right of me. I studied them for a minute. If I waved my arms and jumped around, would someone see me? Would they even realize I needed a rescue?

First things first. I stepped up to the edge where the water was lapping up the sand. "Greg!" I hollered, although it made my throat burn. "GREG!"

Nothing. Even though I watched the air until I had a crick in my neck. Well, this wasn't getting me anywhere right now, and I still wasn't seeing any boats.

Maybe Virgil should add swimming to the list of things he makes me do for training so next time Poseidon decides to drag me off into the deep to force a debt on me I can at least get myself back off whatever island he leaves me on.

I wasn't about to incur any further debts with anyone else by asking them for a ride.

The whispers, figures, shadows and I wandered up the narrow shoreline, keeping close to the water. I didn't want to wander into the middle of the island. I didn't know which one we were on or what was in the trees and undergrowth. I did not need to be fighting my way through that jungle.

"Greg!" I yelled into the air, every so often. I didn't know if he could hear me because I had no idea how far down river I had ended up or what the actual range on his hearing was.

Once we found each other, I might want to rectify that. I paused, thinking. Hopefully he was okay. He had to be okay. And what about the others? Did Ranger get out of the river okay, or had that thing ended up grabbing him too? Or Virgil and Maniac in the warehouse, had Grenadier hit them with an explosive before they made it out?

I was just going to have to trust they were unscathed.

Eventually the shore started to rise, the trees coming right up to the edge of it because it was no longer the sand, but dirt, and I was having to climb over the roots, clinging to branches so I didn't fall into the water itself.

This wasn't going to work because I did not want to be back in that river. I could either go back the way I came and try striking out in the opposite direction to see if I could find a boat on that side of the island, or I could try crossing through the middle. The whispers curled around me, tugging.

"The middle?"

Assent.

"Damn it," I muttered, but I ducked between the trees, picking my way over and crunching through the undergrowth.

When we finally fought free of it, we were on a road. It was not in good shape, the pavement cracked and choked with grass, and in front of us was what looked like a Georgian style house. It too was falling apart, overgrown with leafy green vines.

"Is this supposed to be an improvement?" I asked the whispers. They giggled. "Glad you find this funny," I muttered. They tugged at me again, the figures and shadows flowing toward our left. I sighed and went the direction they wanted me to go, following the road that wound its way down the middle of the island, passing more dilapidated buildings as we went.

The road let out at a small wooden dock. Tied to the dock was one of those little single-engine boats.

The whispers laughed, trilling.

"You want me to take the boat?" They curled against me, the figures brushing my skin and ruffling my hair.

Well, I wasn't arguing the idea, but that boat belonged to someone, and it didn't seem right to leave them stranded. I sat down on the low brick wall that separated the road from the dock itself to wait.

∞

It took a while, based on where the sun was. By the time I actually saw anyone, I would say it was at least close to four or five. I had filled the time by wandering in circles and calling Greg's name repeatedly. It didn't take long for the whispers to get bored of that and fade away.

Hopefully, he could hear me at least faintly so he would know I wasn't somewhere at the bottom of the river. I wasn't sure which way the current had been pulling where we were, so if he had gone searching to make sure I hadn't been pulled out to the sea, he could've gone the wrong direction entirely.

I was focused on that and worried about whether Ranger had gotten out of the harbor too, so I didn't hear anyone until they spoke up behind me.

"You get separated from your group?"

I whirled around, the whispers curling against my shoulders.

The guy took a startled stumble back from me. I could see the panic in his eyes, and I let the whispers go.

"Sorry," I said. "Didn't mean to surprise you."

"Yeah, no, it's cool," he said, rubbing a hand over his shaved head. He looked like he was doing what most people do when the compulsion is so short lived and dismissing his response to the fear as an overreaction. His skin was a warm brown, and he was wearing a bright orange shirt and cargo pants. He had a camera bag slung over one shoulder. "You were calling for someone. You guys get separated?"

"Yeah, looks like I got stranded," I said. What? It's the truth, and this dude didn't need to know how the stranding actually occurred or who was responsible for it.

"Seriously?" he said. "What an asshole. You need a ride? I'm about to head to the main shore."

"That would be great."

He moved around me to head for the boat and then steadied it so I could climb in. He got the engine started, backed the boat away from the dock, and got it turned, and then we were puttering our down the river. Very, very slowly. I wasn't entirely sure we were moving at first.

"I've got to get us down to the docks this way, if that's okay."

I switched positions on the bench I was on, so I was facing him. He seemed nice enough, but experience has taught me that I wanted to be able to see what he was doing. Especially now when I don't know when gods were randomly showing up. "You're the captain."

He smiled at me. "Hardly. It's barely a skipper."

I gave him a tight smile back. Mostly because I'm not big on conversation with strangers to start with. "I wouldn't know. I don't know much about boats."

"Me neither," he said. "I do photography."

"Hey," I said, because I just realized I could've just borrowed his phone rather than endure an uncomfortable boat ride, "you got a phone?" I didn't know which island I had ended up on, but I could've described it to Greg, and I bet Virgil would've known which one it was.

"Yeah."

"Can I use it? I've got a friend waiting on me, and I've got to let him know I'm going to need him to pick me up."

"Sure." He reached into one of the pockets of his pants, slid the phone out and handed it to me. I took a second to think it over. If Greg had gone into the water, would he have had his phone with him? Ranger's would definitely be out of commission.

That left Virgil or Maniac, and I didn't have Maniac's number memorized yet.

I called Virgil. He picked up on the first ring.

"Who is this?"

"It's me! Where's Greg?"

"Meg, Jesus Christ. Greg's still dredging the river, I can't get him to–" he paused, switched subjects. "Where are you?"

"In a boat, somewhere downriver. I got stranded on – what island was that?" I asked the photographer.

"Light Point," he said.

"Light Point Island." Great, it was the hook for a hand serial killer one.

There was a rustle as Virgil pulled the phone away from his face, and I could hear his muffled order. "Ranger! Take the bike, go," the phone was back up at his mouth, his voice clear in my ear. "Which dock is he going to drop you off at?"

"Which dock are we going to?" I asked.

"Pretty Charlotte's."

"Pretty Charlotte's, apparently."

"Ranger! Pretty Char—" and Virgil had hung up. I handed the phone back.

"Thanks," I said.

"No problem. You do this kind of thing often?"

"Do what kind of thing often?"

"Depend on the kindness of strangers."

"No," I said.

"Not much of a damsel in distress?"

"No."

He nodded but seemed to have run out of questions to ask. Despite the noise from the engine, it was now too quiet in the boat.

"What kind of photography do you do?" I asked.

"Abandoned buildings," he said, perking up. "Well, abandoned locations of any kind." He pulled a card out of a different pocket than the one he had stowed his phone in. "Here. This is my website if you ever want to check out any of my work."

I took it and stowed it in my back pocket.

"Here we go," he said, pulling into a dock with several slips for small boats. He bounded out of the boat, reaching back. "Can you toss me the rope? I need to tie it off."

I did as he asked and then climbed out of the boat. I found something I hate more than Ranger or Virgil's driving. Never thought I would have a problem with the slow way.

We headed up the docks and out the entrance to the street. Ranger wasn't here yet.

"So," said the photographer, "do you need me to wait with you?"

"Nope. Thanks for the rescue."

What? I already told you here was no way I was getting off that island on my own unless I had stolen his boat, and I'm not into that. I can admit when it's an actual rescue.

"Any time," he said and trotted off down the street. There was a bus stop just up the corner, so if Ranger didn't get here soon, it wasn't like I didn't have a way to get around.

I sat down on the half wall between the sidewalk and the docks. I had spent most of today just cooling my heels waiting for other people. I was tired, hungry and pissed off, and with pedestrians going up and down the sidewalk, I couldn't have the whispers with me.

I heard the rumbling growl of an approaching motorcycle, and then Ranger was pulling up at the curb and hopping off his bike. He barely had it balanced before he left it, dodging around people, and yanked me up into a hug. He smelled of wet leather and salt water. I could feel my face heat up.

"Um," I said, trying to squirm back.

He pulled back, his hands on my shoulders. "What happened?" he demanded. "I had you and then something, I don't – Jesus, I thought it drowned you."

"I think that was its intention," I said.

He stared at me, his eyes narrowing. "What do you mean that was the intention?"

"It's a long story, and Virgil's going to make me tell it like three more times."

He was still watching me; his hands had tightened briefly. "Meg—" he started, and the look in his eyes made me nervous.

"What happened?" I interrupted him. "Is everyone else okay? Did Grenadier get away again?"

"I'm not telling you until you explain the intentional drowning part."

"Can I *please*," and my voice cracked on the word, "tell this fucking story to everyone all at once?" And I had to swipe at the tears that started.

Ranger looked startled. He pulled me back against him, my face in his chest. "Hey, hey. I'm sorry." He was patting my back. "Everyone's fine. The two of us missed all the action."

I pushed back, and he let go. "How'd you miss the action?"

"I had to wait for a water rescue. And I was busy trying to figure out where that thing had dragged you anyway." He bent at the knees so that his face was level with mine. "Come on, we'll head back over. Virgil might have managed to get Greg's attention by now."

CHAPTER THIRTEEN

It took us a long while to get back over to the abandoned warehouses. Poseidon had dragged me several miles downriver, and we had ended up in a section of outskirt that was south of where I used to live. No wonder Greg couldn't hear me. We had almost the entire city between us.

When Ranger brought the bike onto the main strip of the warehouses, Greg landed in front of it. Ranger had to stop or run into Greg. Since he had just turned onto the street, it at least wasn't a sudden stop, but Greg hadn't actually waited for the bike to come to a stop before he was dodging around it. He almost ended dragging Ranger up with me because it took me a second to release my grip. My arms were shaking – a combination of fatigue and the fact that I hadn't eaten in almost twenty-four hours at this point.

"Meg! Thank God," Greg said, his arms wrapped around me. I could feel the tremor in them. He sounded as exhausted as I felt and seemed only capable of standing there with his nose in my hair. I wasn't sure if it was because he was too tired or relieved to move away from Ranger's bike, since normally he would've scooped me up to fly me wherever we were going. His clothes were still wet, his sweatshirt and my jeans soaking up the water from his shirt and pants. Virgil must have only recently managed to get him out of the harbor.

"What happened?" he asked eventually, when the silence had stretched. It had to have gotten hella awkward for Ranger to sit there watching us.

"She won't say," Ranger said. "Said she needed to be able to tell it once."

Greg's arms tightened around me, the flex of his fingers where they were resting against my shoulder and hip. "It's not good, is it?" he asked me.

"I mean, I didn't die, so we've got that going for us."

"I'm going to be mad, aren't I?"

I hid my face against his chest rather than answer that. I didn't have a choice in the first debt, but I didn't think he was going to be okay with the bargain for the second.

"Meg," he sighed, "right now, I'm just thankful to hear your heart again. I promise not to be mad at you, whatever situation you've gotten into."

"Are we just going to stand here?" Ranger asked. "Because I think Virgil wants us all in the new warehouse."

"What happened to the other one?" I asked, my face still against Greg's chest so it came out muffled.

"Grenadier blew the side up," Greg said. "He had set up with an entire trunk of ammo."

"How'd he find us?"

"Virgil's trying to figure it out. He tossed Maniac's phone into the harbor. She didn't appreciate that."

I snorted. "He'll just give her a new one." Then I thought about it. "Were all the extra phones in the lab?"

"Yes," Greg said. He loosened his grip on me. "Come on, we'll head over. You want to walk?"

"No," I said. "What happened to the Cobra?"

"Ranger reversed the damage on the vehicles. Otherwise, he wouldn't have the bike either." Greg scooped me up. "Come on, we're over on the other side now. Virgil thought it would be better not to be set up next to the water once—" his voice broke, "once we found you."

He launched us up, a huge bounding leap into the air, and then he came down, landing gently in front of a new warehouse labeled A67. Other than the lettering on it, it looked exactly like the last one we were in. Virgil and Maniac were standing out front, the rolling door still all the way up.

"What happened?" Virgil demanded, while Greg was setting me down.

"People keep asking me that," I said. "How about you tell me what happened for a change?"

Maniac snorted. "Virgil and Greg smashed the shit out Grenadier."

"Hmm, yes," Virgil said. "He made a tactical error when he tried to take you and Ranger out first. He must have been watching us for a bit because I think he thought he was looking at Ranger and Maniac. By the time he hit the warehouse itself, we were ready for it."

"Virgil steered one of his rockets back into him. It was awesome," Maniac said.

"Flung it," Virgil said. "I flung it back at him."

"You missed all the fun," Maniac told me.

"Great," I said.

Ranger pulled up, steering his bike past us into the warehouse. He left it just inside, coming back out to us. "So, you caught up?" he asked me.

"Can I have something to eat?" I said. "I spent the first half of the day out of it and the second waiting for a boat captain."

"Our supplies got blown up too," Virgil said, "and they were too full of shards and debris to make it worth trying to fix them. Explain how you ended up on Light Point."

"Poseidon," I said.

"God damn it," Greg said.

"*That's* who tried to drown you? On purpose?" Ranger asked.

"God damn it!" Greg swore again.

"It gets worse," I told him.

"How?" Greg demanded. "How does it get worse?"

"Band-aid," Maniac said. "Just rip it off."

"He let his monster try to drown me so he could save my life and force me into a debt."

Greg shoved his hair back. "How—" he sputtered. "How the fuck does that—" He seemed incapable of finishing the thought.

Virgil was uncharacteristically quiet.

"Not done," I warned Greg. "I owe him twice."

He let go of me, stepping back. "How do you owe him more than once? What could you possibly have—"

"He told me where the Gorgon is," I said. "Well, he gave me a clue."

Greg sounded strangled. "You owe him two debts because he gave you a fucking clue?!" he yelled.

"Don't yell at me!" I shouted back.

"I'm not—" Greg turned away, swearing. "I'm going to rip him apart. Him and his fucking monster."

"What's the price?" Virgil asked.

"He didn't tell me," I said. "Just that one is large, and one is small."

Virgil swore. "So now you owe a god two unknown costs?"

"I didn't get much choice in the matter," I snapped. "I tried not to take what he was offering to start with!"

And Greg heard it in my words, the beat of my heart. "You were going to let yourself drown?"

"We said no bargains."

"Not to that extreme!"

"I didn't know what the cost was going to be! It's life for a life kind of shit here! "

"And we could find a way around the consequences after! We can't do that if you die!" he roared.

"Greg!" Virgil boomed. "Meg! Enough! It's already

done. Arguing over the approach or lack thereof—" and he shot me a stern look, "is not going to get us anywhere."

"That's fine because Greg isn't getting the point anyway," I said.

"What's to get?!" He was yelling again.

"The type of debt this is!" I yelled back. "This isn't just bargaining for information or a hand in hunting someone down! It's a life for a life debt! This is servitude shit! Because he can't die, it's there until he decides that whatever I owe him is satisfied!"

That stunned him into silence.

Oh yeah, I absolutely would've drowned over giving someone, especially a god, that kind of control and leverage over me.

Greg cleared his throat. "We'll find a way around it."

"Will we?" I said.

"Yes," he said, and he sounded so sure about it I almost believed him.

"Future unknown payment aside," Virgil said, "what's the clue for the Gorgon?"

"He's in a cavern by the sea," I said.

"Then we know where he is," Virgil said. "There is only one part of the sewers that size by the harbor."

∞

At this point, we had nothing to sleep on and no food.

But Grenadier was dead. Maniac implied that he was a crispy smear across the alley walls because Greg had crushed him, and then Maniac had lit up what was left.

I didn't want to go confirm it, and any blood that had been on Greg got washed off in the repeated harbor dunkings.

The only reason Virgil, Ranger and Maniac had stayed at the warehouses was because Greg had been frantic, convinced I was still in the water somewhere, and they didn't want to move far in case I showed up. Or if Greg found a body.

They had gotten the vehicles out of the blast radius and repaired while he was in the harbor and then had waited there. Virgil had been trying to talk him into coming out of the water and resting at the point that I had called.

"So," Maniac said, "what're we doing? Because I don't want to sleep on the ground. Or in your car."

Virgil was texting, the only one of us with a surviving phone. Mine had been in the warehouse when it blew up. "I'm getting us a hotel," he said. "With room service."

"Another client?" I asked.

"No. Old friend."

"I feel like your friends and clients have a lot of crossover," I said.

"Tomato-tomatoe," he said. "Okay, we're set. Everyone in the car."

Ranger snorted. "You mean everyone else in the car. I'm not leaving my bike here."

"Would I ask that of you?" Virgil said.

"That depends on what you're—"

"No," Greg said. "Can we just go?" He sounded exhausted, his words almost slurred. We were sitting on the ground, backs against the wall, his arm around me.

To be entirely honest, I wasn't feeling that hot myself, and I hadn't spent the majority of the night and day diving in and out of the harbor, searching the bottom. I had spent most of it unconscious on a beach. That counts as a nap, right?

"Yes," Virgil said. Greg heaved himself up, pulling me with him. He and I climbed into the back, leaving the front for Maniac.

Virgil drove out the garage door, leaving it rolled up even after Ranger followed us.

Greg fell asleep on the way. He had made sure I was buckled in, slung an arm over my shoulder, and then rested his head along his arm, so that my hair was practically in his face. I had tried to shift my curls out of the way, but he had grabbed my hand with his free one and held it the rest of the ride.

When we got to the hotel, Virgil drove straight past the valet, heading into the garage under the building. Not that we should be surprised, since Virgil doesn't let anyone else drive his cars.

I nudged Greg. "We're here."

He raised his head, blinking. "Good." His voice was hoarse. "What's the security like?"

Virgil parked the car. "It's a hotel. It might be five stars, but this isn't villain or god proof."

Greg sighed, climbing out after Maniac and offering me a hand. I took it even though my knee wasn't popping. Ranger parked the bike next to us. We all followed Virgil onto the elevator, and he was back on his phone.

"He's got the suite ready and open for us. We get to skip right past check in," Virgil said, hitting the button for the penthouse.

Greg scrubbed his face. "What's that going to cost us?" I stiffened. He sighed again. "That's not how I meant it, Meg. I meant financials."

Virgil was looking at something else on his phone. "Our operating costs are not looking good. Too much equipment we've got to replace. Some of this is going to end up coming out of pocket."

Greg nodded. "I've got a nest egg I can crack open."

"I thought your clients paid for this stuff," I said.

Virgil chuckled. "No, they pay me a retainer. Technically I'm buying the headquarters apartments from Henry. They don't just supply me with endless gobs of money for no reason. That wouldn't be good business sense."

"If we need to save money, why are we getting an entire suite in this kind of hotel?" I asked pointedly.

"He might be more than an old friend," Virgil said.

I waited, but he didn't elaborate. "What kind of more than an old friend?"

"The kind that will give me this suite for a night for free, for old time's sake."

"That still doesn't explain anything."

"Meg, let it go," Greg said. "It's Virgil's business."

You know me; I have trouble letting go of anything. I'm as bad as Virgil is about badgering and sinking my teeth into something I want answers to, and Virgil hadn't sounded irritated at my questioning, more like he was enjoying dancing around the subject just to frustrate me.

The elevator dinged, and the doors slid open. Virgil herded us all off it, and strode ahead of us through the lobby-like area. With a wave of his hands, the double doors flung themselves open.

There was a man sitting on one of the white couches in the sitting area: salt and pepper beard and hair, dressed in a well-tailored suit and dress shoes. He rose as we came in. "Vigilante," he said in a deep booming voice.

"Craig," Virgil said. "I wasn't expecting the company."

The man's eyes were roving over the rest of us. "I can see that. Not a personal visit then?"

"No."

"A shame," Craig said.

"Indeed," Virgil said, sounding amused.

"Your message was rather vague. So, I had hoped, well – maybe it won't be business next time?"

"I would be amenable to that."

Craig smiled. "Then I'll leave you to it. I've already put in a call to room service; I'll make sure they're aware of the number of people."

"Did you—" Virgil started.

"Vegetarian, as requested," Craig said. "For you or someone on your team?"

"Team member."

"I'll remember that for next time." He gave us a brief nod, and walked past us and out the doors, shutting them behind himself.

Ranger was shedding his jacket, tossing it onto the couch. "How many bathrooms does this place have, or do we need to shower in shifts? I'm tired of smelling like that nasty river water."

"Two," Virgil said. "We've got two bedrooms and then the couches. Meg, I assume you would like one of the bedrooms?"

"Yes, please," I said. I would be sharing it with Greg anyway.

"The exposure risk is the same for all the rooms," Virgil said, and I knew it was for Greg's sake. "I'm going to put the two of you in the east side bedroom. Maniac, you're in the west. Ranger and I can take the couches to guard the doors."

"I should—" Greg protested.

"No, no, you should not. You've spent the better part of twenty-four hours pushing yourself past your limits." Greg had opened his mouth to protest again, and Virgil rode right over the top of whatever Greg had been about to say. "Yes, even you have limits, Greg. Shower, eat, rest. In that order. Because tomorrow we have a Gorgon to kill."

Greg sighed again and gave my hand a tug, leading me to the room on the left, and he closed the French doors to it behind us. He scrubbed at his face. "Do you want to shower first?"

"No," I said, pulling off his sweatshirt and my shirt underneath together in one go. "I want to shower with you."

"Meg," he said, but there was relief in his voice, and he pulled me back against him, his lips on mine. His hands were on my waist before he moved one to my hair. I stepped backwards, leading him, while I pulled my jeans down. He caught me before I could trip over the fabric clinging to my legs. He chuckled, peeling them the rest of the way off, freeing me from the material before he stood back up and removed his own shirt. He pulled me back against his chest, his arms wrapped around me, nose in my hair.

"I love you," he said. "I'm sorry I yelled at you."

"Do we have to discuss that right now?" I asked. "Because all I want is to get this sand out of my hair."

"Is that really all you want?' he asked, his breath tickling my ear. "You're just using me to wash your curls?"

"No," I said, and I kissed him. He chuckled again, lips against mine and lifted me up, carrying me the rest of the way to the bathroom, where he shut and locked that door and got the shower started.

We got around to washing my hair eventually.

CHAPTER FOURTEEN

"Your power permeates the world," she said as we sat beneath a tree in our olive grove, backs against the trunks. We could hear the sea, the wind bringing the sound of the crashing waves to our ears. "Without it...well, perhaps."

"Perhaps?" we asked.

"Perhaps things would not be as they are," she said.

"What could loss of our power possibly change?" we asked, but she had vanished.

∞

Virgil let us all sleep late. Probably because there hadn't been much conversation from any of us once we had food in the suite. We had eaten single-mindedly, and then Greg and I had gone back to our room. He had pulled me to him, his chest pressed to my back, curled up around me as much as he could be, and fallen asleep as soon as he had stopped moving.

It had taken me a while longer than that to fall asleep, as tired as I was. I was worried about why Poseidon would've gone so far out of his way to make sure I was tied to whatever plans he had. Whatever it was he wanted, he must have been sure I would've refused to help with it if I had any other choice.

It must be something big if he thought I would risk offending him. He might not be Zeus, but he wasn't someone I wanted to piss off.

Plus side: Bacchus and Ares were keeping the fact that the Furies weren't up to snuff to themselves, since everyone seemed surprised that I wasn't operating on the same level as them. Eventually they would all know, but that was a problem for the future.

When I woke up, Greg was still wrapped around me, and I needed to stretch my legs out. He sat up before I could try shifting, and when I turned my head to look up at him, he settled a hand against my face, his thumb brushing my cheek.

"Hi," I said.

"Hi," he said.

"How long have you been awake?"

"Long enough."

"You didn't want to go get coffee?"

His expression was worried. "And let you out of my sight?"

"You'd be one room over," I said. "You know Virgil's probably already got room service up here. Bet you Craig sent him something special."

He smiled at me, but it didn't reach his eyes. "Meg, I don't know if I can keep doing this."

I shot up, almost clocking him in the chin, which would've hurt me a lot more than him. "Doing what?" I said, my voice shrill, panicked.

"No, not like that!" he said. "Never like that."

"Then don't say it like that!" I said, my heart still hammering. He pulled me against him, his nose in my hair.

"If I retired, would you come with me?" he asked when I had finally calmed down.

I squirmed back. "I won't ask you to do that." I knew what he was offering, and he wouldn't be happy with that life. Well, maybe for a little while, but eventually he would regret it. He couldn't just set aside the hero inside; it was apparently something he and his father had in common. And now, I was too far in and didn't want to leave it either. Longings for normalcy and quiet aside. The realization gave me pause, to know that I was choosing to stay in a life I had avoided for so long, and I had to mull it over for a moment, registering that when it came down to it, I knew which road I would prefer.

Better a hero, well, kind of a hero, than a villain.

He made a frustrated noise. "I know you won't. But now you owe a god an unknown level of debt. Because he tried to drown you to start with. I don't know how to keep you safe from them."

"Retiring will definitely not help with that," I told him. "They'll just find me anyway. We'll have gods popping into the garden asking for cups of tea."

"Have you been watching *Sarah and Duck* again?" he asked, pulling back.

"No," I lied.

"*Mary Poppins?*" He had decided not to call me on it.

"Nope."

"*Wallace and Gromit?*" Oh, he was just going to let this keep going.

"Uh uh," I said, "and that would be cheese anyway."

He chuckled. "Did you happen to watch all three in a row?"

"Absolutely not." I took a break in between the episodes at least. And *Mary Poppins* was on a totally different day.

He put his hand back on my face. "We will solve this. I'm not going to let them just push you around."

"I don't let anyone push me around," I said. I would have to find some way to slide out of whatever my debt was.

"I feel like this is one of those cases where they'll just keep changing the playing field and the game on us."

There was a knock at the door. Greg sighed, grumbled. "Timing." It was half-hearted at best.

Virgil popped the lock and stuck his head through the

door. "Are you two done? We're all very aware of the 'don't let the gods push Meg around plan'. It's going to have to go on the backburner."

Greg scrubbed at his face. "What's the plan?" he asked, apparently deciding to just get down to business.

"The plan is to eat, get dressed, retrieve the swords and Meg's outfit, and then we need to get new compacts."

"Compacts?" Greg asked.

"Little folding mirrors," Virgil said. "Women – scratch that – people use them for things like applying makeup. They are the most practical item available for this."

"I know what they are," Greg said irritably. "I thought we were trying to go as hands-free as possible."

"Yes, well, it wasn't feasible in the way I wanted and with the time we had, let alone have now." He stared at us for a minute. "Are you two getting up?"

"When you close the door," Greg said. "Our clothes stink, by the way."

"That might actually be a point in our favor," Virgil said. "We don't know what kind of sense of smell the Gorgon has, so smelling like the harbor might be for the best." He pulled his head out, shutting the door.

Greg sighed again, levering himself up out of the bed, snagging our clothes off the floor. He handed mine over to me before he started pulling his on.

The clothes smelled worse than they had yesterday if that was even possible. Or maybe it was because I had gotten used to the scent while I was wearing them. I wrinkled my nose but got up and put them on anyway. Unless I was planning on riding back over to our apartments naked, I didn't have much choice.

Well, I guess I could steal one of the bathrobes, but Craig would probably have a problem with that.

Over breakfast there was some arguing over whether it would be safe to leave Ranger's bike here. Virgil won when he made the point that if Ranger did get injured badly enough that he couldn't drive it, that would mean his bike would be left completely unguarded. At least leaving it here meant he knew where to find it.

In the end, all five of us squeezed into the Cobra. Maniac, Ranger and I were in the back, with me sandwiched between the two of them. Greg ground his teeth over that, but Ranger's not as bulky as Greg, and I was the only one small enough to fit in what passes for a middle seat in that thing.

When we got to the apartments, Virgil illegally parked at the curb, and sent Greg in to get our stuff. Greg had just gone straight up to the roof, disappearing over the edge of the building.

Virgil was drumming his fingers on the steering wheel, an uncommon expression of impatience from him.

"You got a problem?" Ranger asked.

"We have too many problems," Virgil said.

"We should take some time off after this," Ranger said. "The gods won't be going anywhere."

Virgil twisted to face us. "Excuse me? Who's going to deal with any monsters that pop up while we're gone?"

Maniac snorted. "Let the military deal with it. I don't know why we're the only ones handling Hydras to start with. Maybe those assholes should be doing their jobs."

"I believe they're unaware of the scope of the issue at hand," Virgil said.

"You going to be the one to tell them?" Ranger asked.

Virgil was silent.

"Didn't think so," Ranger said. "You don't want them mucking around and red taping us anymore than I do, and you know they would."

Greg was knocking on the passenger side window. "Pop the trunk," he said. Virgil did as he asked, and Greg set the case that held the swords in it along with my suit before he came back around and climbed into the car. "Landlord's going to be pissed. I had to rip off his new door to the roof."

"You couldn't just pop the lock?" Virgil said.

"He had it padlocked on the inside," Greg said, "so no."

"Seems like an unnecessary precaution to take when there's a hole in the side of the building." Virgil said.

"Couldn't you have just gone in through what was left of the lab?" I asked.

"Could've, but I didn't," Greg said. "He's got plastic sheeting up over it anyway."

Virgil had pulled away from the curb and headed back in the direction of the harbor. "We're going to stop off and get the mirrors. Greg, you running in?"

"Where are we going?"

Virgil was scrolling through his phone, the car seemingly steering itself. "There's an ULTA on the way."

"Watch the road!" Ranger said, reaching forward to slow cars as we went barreling through a red light.

"I saw them," Virgil said.

"Then why I am the one handling them?" Ranger said.

"Because you had a free hand," Virgil said.

"Why are we going to UTLA?" Maniac asked. "I don't think the Gorgon is going to care about how good our makeup is."

"For compacts, so we have a reflective surface," Virgil said.

"Don't see how that's going to help."

"It's how Perseus defeated him to start with," I said. "He, or well, she, according to Ares, used a mirrored shield to sneak up on him while he was sleeping and cut his head off."

"Huh," Maniac said.

"Greg? Or I can send Meg in," Virgil said.

"No, I've got it."

"I can go into a store," I protested.

Greg twisted in the seat. "Meg. We know you can go into a store. It'll be faster just to send me."

I glared at him for a moment, then switched subjects. "What about lights?"

"We're just going to use the flashlight on my phone,"

Virgil said. "It's bright enough, and you're going to be the one holding it."

"Why me?"

"Because you're taking point," Virgil said.

"No," Greg said. "I should be point."

"No, you shouldn't."

"I'm the—"

"I know what your skills are. Meg is taking point with the Furies because they will lead her where we need to go."

I may or may not have looked entirely too smug at that point because the look on Greg's face did not bode well regarding lack of arguments for either of us.

But I had a thought. "If the Furies will lead us, how come I wasn't included on the recon team?"

"Because we didn't know which cavern we needed to be in. Would they have helped us navigate for the ones that didn't have the Gorgon?"

"Probably not," I admitted. We stayed silent for the rest of the trip. Although I could hear Greg grinding his teeth.

∞

So, you know how on TV, the sewers are *huge*? Like, there's nice walkways above the sewage, and plenty of space for standing straight up, and at least five feet of clearance still above your head?

Yeah, no. They're not like that in real life.

I mean, there was enough space to stand, but the section that we were going into was quite literally one long tube, and we were going to be walking through water.

We had picked up mirrors, which at this point I wasn't sure were going to be any use, but Virgil assured me there would be corners, and before we went down into the manhole, I had stayed in the back of the Cobra to get that stupid catsuit on and then back into my clothes. I don't think there's a point to it against the Gorgon, but Greg had insisted.

Fortunately, the Gorgon was in the storm sewer system, not the sewage.

Once we were in the sewer tunnel itself, Greg protested again, because with the lack of overall space, I would have to be sure to get out of the way for anyone else to move forward. Virgil had overridden it by outright ignoring him.

"Meg, call them. Figure out if we're going left or right," Virgil said. The three of them backed up while Ranger stayed next to me. He had one of the swords propped on his shoulder like he would his bat.

The whispers tugged me to the right, away from Virgil, Maniac and Greg. I started off, the figures and shadows sliding across the walls and through the air, whispers riding my shoulders, sighing in my ears. I ended up handing Virgil's phone to Ranger, the flashlight set as low as it would go, and Ranger shined it at my feet so we could see where we were stepping.

With the whispers, I didn't need the light anyway. Plus, it's a tunnel. What is there to trip on? It's not like when we were in the subway and needed to worry about the tracks or falling off the walkway.

Our footsteps and the sound of water splashing echoed in the small space. I knew that was making us all tense because we were trying to walk quietly. The figures and I were both running our fingers down the walls, theirs scratching against the concrete.

"Can you make them stop that?' Ranger whispered up at me. His voice echoed strangely, bouncing off the walls and making it much louder than he meant. I heard Virgil wince.

The figures pulled their fingers away from the walls and dragged them through the water instead, creating little waves and wake as we went. It was better than the noise they had been making. The fact that they did it because Ranger asked gave me pause because they did it before I said anything to them. I turned my head to look back at him, and he gave me a thumbs up and mouthed thanks. I flicked my eyes off him and over to Greg who also looked relieved that they had stopped, so I wasn't sure who they had responded to.

Eventually we came to a T in the system. Ranger grabbed my arm and tried to slip past me, but when I grabbed him back, he paused long enough for me to pull out a compact and get the mirror open and pointed while he held the flashlight up and around the corner to the right. We repeated it for the left side even though the whispers were tugging me to the right again.

We slowly made our way, checking around corners, following the tug of the whispers, ears straining for any noise other than that of our feet, the water and the figures' fingers when they would forget and scratch at the walls again. I suppose none of us needed to worry about hearing anything else since Greg would warn us if he heard the Gorgon moving around; still, we were tense and expectant. The sound of rushing water was slowly getting louder.

Finally, the tunnel spit us out into the cavern-like space that we were looking for. Calling it a cavern was generous; it was more like a sort of medium-sized cave, and here was the waterfall of water we had been hearing echoing up the sewers. It was pounding down into a pool of water at the bottom, and any of the concrete spaces on either side of it and the river working its way into another tunnel were empty.

I stepped into it without thinking, following the tug of the whispers, and Ranger jerked me back. From the light, I had seen enough to know there was nothing there, so I shook his hand off.

"It's not there," I said, the whispers still pulling. "I think we need to go further in."

"Can you have them go?" Virgil said. "I want to see if there's anywhere we can hunker down and wait so we can ambush it when it comes back."

Caution, they told me, when I said they could go, *it's near.* "They're telling me it's nearby," I said to Virgil.

"All the more reason to make this quick," Virgil said

211

before he, Maniac and Greg all made their way past me and the entrance into the tunnel once the whispers had gone. Ranger stayed back by me, shining the flashlight up.

Unless we wanted to get into the water and try to stay under the waterfall, there was nowhere in the cavern itself to hide. Virgil made an irritated noise. "We can't just stay back in the tunnel; we don't know which direction it will be coming from."

Greg was studying the space, having stepped up to the water's edge. "It's not even tall enough that I could stay up at the top to stay hidden. The water is going to be our only choice."

"Well we need to make a decision—" Virgil stopped because Greg had waved his hand at him, a shushing movement.

"Something doesn't sound—" his brow was furrowed, head cocked to the side as he tried to focus on the noise attracting his attention. His head came up, a look of alarm on his face. "It's in the water!"

The water erupted, raining down on us as the Gorgon surged up out of it. I ducked back, scrambling to the side as it came crashing down. Would've been nice if Poseidon had bothered to mention the fucking thing was a water moccasin.

The startled yell from Greg and the crack of concrete as the Gorgon's body hit it were the only things that made me turn back to see what was going on. Otherwise I might have had the forethought to remember I was holding a small mirror and could look behind me that way.

The Gorgon had Greg on the ground, attempting to pry his arms almost lovingly off his face, its own face hovering over Greg's, hissing in multiple voices, snakes writhing along its head and down its neck and back like a crest. The whispers and I screamed, figures rushing forward at it, fingers scrabbling up its stone skin.

The Gorgon looked up. I had done what I intended and attracted his attention. But now I met his eyes, and the whispers howled as they, the figures and the shadows turned to dust, their physical forms scattering across the sewer floor. I could still feel them in the ether, but my relief was short-lived because in that moment I felt it: the hardening of my skin, traveling up my hand, down along my shoulder, and I couldn't tear my eyes free.

Maniac had rushed forward, flames streaming across Greg and the Gorgon, the water hissing as the heat hit it and it evaporated. I could hear the concrete crack again, but still I was frozen as the stone worked its way up my neck; I could feel it on my legs.

Ranger tackled me, knocking me to the ground and breaking the spell I had been trapped in. "Fuck," he said, and then again. "Fuck, Meg, don't move."

I couldn't answer him that I wasn't sure I could move anyway. It felt like my jaw had already sealed shut. We were surrounded by gusting wind, and as Ranger reversed what the Gorgon had done, it hurt as if my skin was tearing away. I couldn't scream at first, only make desperate whimpers as I lay there.

With one, giant ripping sensation, the feeling of being frozen in place left as I howled, and once it passed, I was left panting, staring at the ceiling of the sewer. Ranger yanked me up, shoving me toward a wall, and he left me there. I could hear his footsteps headed back to the battle.

"Keep its head down!" I could hear Greg roaring.

"I fucking know!" Virgil yelled back. "I can't look at it!"

Can't meet the eyes of something you can't see to begin with. Virgil's phone had gotten dropped on the concrete, the flashlight up, and the whispers were clamoring to come back. When I called to them, the figures swept the phone into the water. Virgil was going to be pissed because I could've just turned the flashlight off. The only light left was the flames from Maniac's hands.

"Maniac!" I yelled. "Stop!"

"Are you insane?!" she yelled. The Gorgon was rearing,

hissing and spitting; it couldn't get near her because of the heat.

"It'll just hide in the water if you don't!" I yelled back, that being the only thing I could think of to get her to listen.

The flames stopped, and we were plunged into darkness.

The scraping of stone on concrete and the menace of the hissing voices continued, but now Greg had the advantage, and I heard the thing shriek in surprise as he slammed into it. I could hear its tail thrashing, hitting the water with explosive force as it tried to retreat backwards, but Greg was dragging it forward, yelling.

"Here! Virgil, here, pin it!"

"Should've brought a jackhammer," Ranger said.

Greg grunted, his only response, and then the clanging of metal on stone, a clatter as the sword hit the floor. "Blade broke."

The Gorgon was shrieking, screaming, still struggling against Virgil and Greg who, from the sound of it, had its head pinned to the ground.

"Ranger, slow its back end!" Greg was shouting again.

"Maniac, concentrate the flames. I need you to melt out its neck," Virgil's voice, calm and steady.

"Sweet," Maniac said. "I love having an excuse to do this." A white flame appeared in the center of one of her palms, fierce and bright, narrow like a welding torch would be. "Oh, don't look right at it," she said belatedly.

I could see again, though, despite having ducked my head so I wasn't looking at the flame in Maniac's hand. Greg and Virgil were at its head and shoulders, Virgil palms out, hovering over the head, its face pushed onto the floor, Greg bent, pushing down against the shoulders, his chest pressed to the thing's back, the snakes on it curling around his arms and neck, hissing in his ears. The Gorgon's claws were scrabbling at the ground. Maniac stepped up to it and pressed the flame to the thing's neck.

It wailed. Unearthly and strange, I could feel it in my bones, the hairs on the back of my neck rising. Through the noise it made, Maniac persisted even though her shoulders hunched, and I could tell she wanted to step away from it even as I fought the urge to back up.

The stone of its neck bubbled up, dripping and melting, it's struggles slowly ceasing, until finally the head broke free, the body sagging. Virgil pulled the head away from the body and set it down so that the eyes faced the wall.

"Melt the head too," he said. Maniac complied until all that was left was a glowing red puddle of stone on the floor.

Greg ripped himself free of the snakes that lined the Gorgon's body. Once the Gorgon had gone down, they had stopped moving as well, but because they were stone, they didn't just loosen, they had stayed wrapped around him. They crumbled and hit the concrete in rattling pieces.

Maniac had changed the flames back to the cooler temperature of orange and yellow, holding her hand aloft like a torch. Virgil was looking around. "Where's my phone?" he asked.

"Gorgon knocked it into the water," I lied. Both Virgil and Greg shot me looks. "Okay, fine, the Furies kicked it into the water instead of letting me turn it off."

"You okay?" Greg asked me.

"Totally fine," I said.

He eyed me for a minute. "Why'd you scream?"

"I knocked her down and made her face the wall," Ranger said. "She didn't appreciate that."

Greg grunted. I, for one, was grateful that Ranger covered for me and spared Greg the stress over my almost-petrification.

Virgil had a hand over the water, and his phone came shooting up. He sighed, looking at it. "Ranger, can you reverse the damage to this?"

"Hand it over," Ranger said, taking the phone. A gust of wind, and he handed it back to Virgil.

"Thank you. Now, is everyone still alive? Unharmed? Good, let's go."

The mood on the way out was much more jovial and louder than on the way in.

"Time off?" Ranger asked as we climbed out the manhole.

"Fine," Virgil said. "I need to find us a new temporary base anyway."

"Oh no, no, you're coming with us," Ranger said.

"For what?"

"Team building exercise," Ranger said.

∞

Ranger had insisted on taking all of us camping in the Catskill Mountains. He refused to answer me on whether those woods actually contain bears. I don't know what he said to convince Greg that it was a great idea because I had loudly, insistently, protested. Several times.

Maniac said as long as we packed enough snacks, and maybe some drinks for shots, she was game for anything.

Virgil's Humvee order wasn't in yet, so he had borrowed the Jeep with the missing doors since we needed a vehicle with storage for all the camping paraphernalia and space to fit us. I don't know who thought it was a good idea to remove all four doors to start with.

Once I was sitting out on the beach by a lake while the sun set, and Maniac got the campfire going, I had to admit Ranger's idea wasn't totally horrible. We had tents, cots, sleeping bags, cooking ware, even a coffee pot so that we could brew coffee in the morning, although it required some extra work if Maniac wasn't awake to handle fire duty yet.

It was a good, relaxing sort of week, and I spent most of it by the lake itself.

Right? You would think I'd be avoiding all water.

Greg joined me on the shore, easing himself down onto the sand before he wrapped an arm around my waist. I leaned into him. He kissed my head and was silent for a moment.

216

"Think that'll be the last of the monsters?" he asked eventually.

"I don't know," I said truthfully. He was silent again while we watched the waves lapping at the beach.

"I don't want to wait for Sandra and Brit to get things planned," he said. "When we get back to town, I want to go straight to the courthouse and get married."

"What about your mom?" I asked. "Won't she be mad?"

"She'll have to get over it," he said.

"I think Sandra and Brit are going to be disappointed," I said.

"They'll have to get over it too."

"Tony will never let you hear the end of it."

"Meg," he said, and he sounded exasperated. "Since when do you care about disappointing other people?"

"I care about disappointing you," I said. His arm around me tightened.

"I love you," he said. "And I don't want—I just want that permanence between us. I don't want you to ever doubt my feelings for you, in case—" he paused, took a breath, "just in case." He went silent, staring out at the water, and I knew that there were words left unsaid, and it made me scared of what he may be planning.

Could – would – gods transfer the debt owed to another carrier?

Well, if Greg thought he could get Poseidon to lift my debt and move it to his shoulders, he better have another thought coming because I wouldn't let him do that. Not because I don't let Greg come to my rescue that way but because I don't know that whatever task Poseidon would make him perform wouldn't break him.

I won't let a god force Fortress to compromise his morals for Vengeance.

But all I said was, "Okay."

"Okay?"

"Okay," I said, and Greg kissed me.

There was a shout from farther down the shore. Maniac was yelling at Ranger who had kicked water up at her, and she chased him further into the lake. They both went under the water and came up sputtering and laughing.

From behind us came the ringing of a cowbell, and Greg winced, covering his ears.

"Dinner!" Virgil said, ringing the bell again.

"I'm going to crush that thing into a ball," Greg said. I snorted, giggling. Virgil had been ringing it for every meal since we got here.

Dinner was trout that Virgil had pulled out of the lake. Ranger called it cheating to the extreme; Virgil called it practical application of skill.

Since it was our last night, Ranger had pulled out marshmallows, graham crackers and chocolate bars he had squirreled away somewhere. How he managed to keep those supplies hidden from all of us I don't know since we had all assisted in packing and unpacking the food and camping gear.

I ended up going to bed earlier than everyone else, falling asleep to the sound of their voices and laughter.

I woke up with Greg's hand on my back and the noise of a drum like a rattle in my ears. Something walked by the tent. For a moment, I held my breath, but Greg stayed asleep, another instant where REM trumps super hearing.

I slipped out from under Greg's hand, unzipped and stepped out of the tent barefoot, into the light of the moon. There were stars above me and the sound of the water ahead of me. The campfire had burnt down to sullen embers, spots of orange and red in the night.

Even the crickets had ceased.

There was a peacock on the shore, and beside him, a woman: tall, willowy, her hair up in a chignon bun. She half-turned and motioned for me to come to her.

Cautiously, the whispers, figures, shadows and I flowed forward, darkening the ground we tread on, chasing the moonlight away from us, until we stood beside her at the water's edge.

"Megaera," she said, her voice melodious.

"Hera," we said. The peacock turned to face us, the eyes in his tail blinking. He rattled them again as he furled and unfurled the feathers.

"My husband is looking for you," she said, having turned back to the water.

"We won't go to him," the whispers and I said. "Never again will we do his bidding."

She turned her head back to face us. There was a gleam of something in her eyes, cold and blue. "You may find your— willing – compliance is not required from him."

"We know what we risk."

She tilted her head to the side, considering, then reached forward. The whispers and I tried to step backwards, but her hand was on my chin, capturing my face, and we were frozen, stilled as she looked us in the eyes. "In that case, I give you my blessing." Her power spouted, heavy in the air, and it was filled with the scent of lilies. When I breathed it in, I could feel it rushing into my lungs, spilling outward, racing through my veins.

I was left alone on the sand, the smell of her flowers lingering on my skin, the fading sensation of hooks sinking into my heart, stinging with every beat. For a moment, I was alarmed, and then the thought slid away before it fully formed, and I couldn't remember why I was worried to start with.

I have got to stop wandering off on my own. It never results in anything good.

"Meg!" Greg was coming out of the tent, moving hurriedly down to me. "What are you doing?"

"I couldn't sleep," I said. I couldn't tell him there had been a goddess here. He was worried about me enough, and it was truth enough that he might not hear that there was more to it. He stopped in front of me, the concern on his face clear in the moonlight, the brightness of the stars. I rose up on my toes and kissed him, and he responded, his hands slipping under my shirt, fingers skimming across my skin.

When I twined my arms around his neck, he lowered us both to the sand.

He failed to notice the extra sets of footprints that had been left on the shore.

ABOUT THE AUTHOR

Jamie lives in Charlotte, NC with her husband, three feral children and two badly behaved dogs.

She has BAs in English and Theatre, her favorite part of which was working backstage on traveling Broadway productions.

www.ingramcontent.com/pod-product-compliance
Lightning Source LLC
Chambersburg PA
CBHW020940180626
46814CB00003B/883